# THE MISSING VIDEO

## Dave Gustaveson

YWAM Publishing
A Ministry of Youth With A Mission
P.O. Box 55787, Seattle, WA 98155
(206) 771-1153

YWAM Publishing is the publishing ministry of Youth With A Mission. Youth With A Mission (YWAM) is an international missionary organization of Christians from many denominations dedicated to presenting Jesus Christ to this generation. To this end, YWAM has focused its efforts in three main areas: 1) Training and equipping believers for their part in fulfilling the Great Commission (Matthew 28:19). 2) Personal evangelism. 3) Mercy ministry (medical and relief work).

For a free catalog of books and materials write or call:
YWAM Publishing
P.O. Box 55787, Seattle, WA 98155
(206)771-1153 or (800) 922-2143
email adress: 75701.2772 @ compuserve.com

**The Missing Video**

Published by Youth With A Mission Publishing
P.O. Box 55787
Seattle, WA 98155

ISBN 0-927545-60-8

**Printed in the United States of America.**

To my daughters
Jamie Leah
and
Katie Lanae,
and all the other kids
who can dream of
what might
be.

Other

**REEL KIDS**
Adventures

Available at your local Christian bookstore or
YWAM Publishing
1(800) 922-2143

# Acknowledgments

When I got the idea for this book, the flicker of creativity would have been snuffed out unless key people kept it alive. No one writes a book alone. I want to honor some of those special people who helped me.

I thank God for my wife, Debbie, who kept encouraging me to write down ideas from bedtime stories I told my kids. Special love to my daughters, Jamie and Katie, who always begged for more.

I thank Loren Cunningham and my dear friends in Youth With A Mission. My long years in YWAM have given me a deep reservoir from which to draw. A person can't write unless he has something to say. I pray that the values and principles I've learned over the years will challenge kids around the world.

Special thanks to Jim and Jan Rogers, who kept me moving. Thanks to Merry Hofmann and Pam Warren for their special insights; to Tom Bragg and Warren Walsh for their tireless work at YWAM Publishing; and to Dave Dickson for his insights on Cuba. I'm grateful for my friend John Dawson, who is a very gifted writer. His encouragement was a blessing.

God's gift to any author are editors who live to make writers look better. Shirley Sells is such a servant. She is committed to what she puts her hand to, and spent long hours making this story come alive.

And without God's grace, none of this could have been possible. Thanks, Lord, for changing my life.

May this book inspire a host of kids to give their lives to Jesus and to world evangelism.

# Table of Contents

# Chapter 1

# Running Out of Time

Two days to go. Jeff Caldwell stared at the number 8 circled in red on his calendar.

It was already Thursday, April 6.

"Cuba," he said out loud. Funny. It had sounded so exciting when he first heard about the trip. He had dreamed of running on the beaches in Havana, weaving between palm trees, lying in the sun—almost impossible dreams now.

With just two days left, the group's visas still hadn't come through. They had known the process wouldn't be easy, but it almost seemed impossible for them to get the visas now.

Jeff sat on his bed in his faded jeans and T-shirt, and ran his fingers through his curly blond hair. He shook his head, dreading the moment he had to tell the news to his sister.

Jeff's sister, Mindy, was 13 and had just gotten braces. He'd called her "metal mouth" until his parents put a stop to it. When Jeff was little, he couldn't pronounce Melinda, so he called her Mindy, and the nickname stuck.

Mindy burst into Jeff's room, a wide grin framing her metal-laced teeth.

"Well, are we going or what?" she shouted, bobbing up and down. Her pale yellow ponytail rose and fell with each jump. She leaned over until her intense brown eyes were almost even with his blue ones.

"Hold on a minute, Mindy," Jeff said. "We're working on it."

Slowly rising from his bed, Jeff put a hand on each of her shoulders. Although he was only 15, he was already seven inches taller than Mindy, and seemed to tower over her. He looked down at his little sister sadly.

"Mindy, I'll be honest with you. There's not much time left, and we still haven't gotten the visas. I don't honestly know what's gonna happen."

Tears welled in Mindy's eyes. She took off her brown-rimmed glasses and set them on his bed. "I wish I'd never heard of dumb ol' Cuba. Or your club, either."

*If wishes worked, we'd be on the plane right now,* Jeff thought. He placed no faith in wishes. Wishes, no;

prayers, yes. He wondered why his prayers hadn't been answered.

"Hang in there," he said, with more assurance than he felt, and handed Mindy a tissue to blot the tears slipping down her cheeks. "God's always come through for us before."

"Well, if this doesn't work out, don't ask me to go next time. I've been packed for a week, just waiting."

Jeff glanced at his watch nervously. It was almost 7:30 a.m. They had been excused from first period study hall, but they'd still have to hurry to see the travel agent and still make their second-period class.

Jeff heard about the Reel Kids Adventure Club right after his family moved to Los Angeles and he enrolled in Baldwin Heights High School. It sounded like fun, so he signed up.

Warren Russell, head of the school's communications department, came up with the idea for the club as a way to take high school kids on trips to different countries. They could use their communications skills and share their faith at the same time.

The club met off campus, but had permission to use school equipment. The idea was to produce videos of their adventures and show them to youth groups at local churches. They hoped to inspire the churches to send out teams of their own.

Jeff saw only one drawback. After he went with Warren on a few short trips to "scout out the land," Mindy wanted to join the club. Jeff didn't want her tagging along, but didn't have much choice. His parents had practically insisted. Finally, he gave in and Mindy joined the club. She had been so excited about going on the first trip for the whole club. But now....

Jeff punched Mindy's arm playfully. "Warren better show up soon. We've only got two hours before we have to be at school."

"I think I hear a car," she said, and Jeff ran to the window just in time to see Warren's blue station wagon pulling up.

"Mindy, get your books. I'll meet you outside," he said, grabbing his books and heading out the door. He ran toward the car, hoping to talk to Warren alone before Mindy got there.

"Anything new, Warren?" he asked, jerking open the door.

Mr. Russell had given the team members permission to call him "Warren" when they were away from school. He was only in his early 30s and looked even younger, so he was often confused with one of his students. Warren was still single, and the Reel Kids Adventure Club was the love of his life.

"Nothing yet," he replied glumly.

Mindy was right behind Jeff. Her long legs and persistence enabled her to keep up with him almost everywhere he went. She could tell by their faces that there was no need to ask dumb questions.

While he buckled his seat belt, Jeff sighed. "Why do you think we're having so much trouble, Warren?"

"I don't know. After we pick up K.J., we'll stop by the travel agent and see how it's going."

Jeff clutched his books to his chest. It was bad enough to disappoint his sister, but having to face K.J. was going to be even worse. K.J. had wanted so much to be a part of the group. He'd worked hard to become a good cameraman so they'd take him along.

"I talked to my pastor last night," Warren said, "and he was able to set up a few services for us in Cuba. And they're working on more. We'll talk to them once we get there."

"Well, that's one less thing to worry about," said Jeff. "Now all we have to do is get there!"

"Did K.J. get his money yet?" Mindy asked as they turned onto K.J.'s street.

"Not the last time I heard. He's paid for the trip to Mexico, but still needs $450 for the trip to Cuba. We need him. There's no time to replace him now."

Mindy leaned forward. "I hope he goes. He's funny."

"Yeah. Sometimes too funny," Jeff muttered.

Kyle James Baxter was already waiting in front of his house. He was 14, but was only 5' 6", three inches shorter than Jeff. He was always ready to try something new, often getting into trouble in the process. He jumped into the back seat next to Mindy.

"Everything set?" he asked hopefully. Three heads shook.

K.J. tried to cheer them up. "Hey, did you see the cartoon about our principal in the high school paper?" He burst out laughing. "Pretty funny, huh?"

"I thought it was great," Mindy said. "You don't know who drew it, do you?" she asked mischievously. She and K.J. grinned at each other.

"Did you get your money yet?" Warren changed the subject.

"Not yet. I'll have to pull out if something doesn't come through soon. My mom's still trying to get my dad to help out. But we don't see him that often," K.J. said, pulling a comb through his thick, dark hair.

"Has he been over lately?" Mindy asked.

"Oh, yeah. Just the other day. He says I'm crazy for spending my spring break in Cuba."

"Well, at least your mom is behind you. And she's not even a Christian."

Warren maneuvered through the early morning traffic while Jeff sat quietly trying to sort out his thoughts and Mindy and K.J. laughed and jabbed each other in the back seat.

As soon as Warren parked in front of the travel agency, he turned to Jeff. "Before we go in, would you say a prayer for us?"

Jeff turned to look at Mindy and K.J. "Before I do," he said, "I need to get something off my chest. I really didn't like it when Warren asked you two to go on this trip. I thought you couldn't cut it. Maybe my attitude's why we're having such a hard time now. Maybe it's my fault."

"Well, then, just maybe I shouldn't go," K.J. snapped, his dark eyes reflecting his hurt.

"No! The problem is mine, not yours," Jeff said. Then he bowed his head and said, "Lord, You know we've had our hearts set on going on this trip. But Lord, I give this trip to You. If You want us to go, make a way for it to happen."

"Amen," K.J. said. "Amen," Mindy and Warren echoed loudly.

# Chapter 2

# Is No News Good News?

Do you think he'll have our visas?" Mindy asked Warren as soon as they sat down in the waiting area.

"We'll know in just a few minutes."

"I still don't see what the big problem is. Have you ever had this much trouble getting into other countries?"

"Yes. But not this close to departure time. God must have something special in mind."

"What do you mean?"

Warren turned his head slightly toward Mindy. "The tougher the battle, the greater the victory."

He said, "The problem is that we're Americans."

"What's that got to do with anything?"

"Their government hasn't been on speaking terms with ours since 1961. They're used to thinking that most Americans are spies."

"Well, other Americans are going there," Mindy persisted.

Warren swiveled slightly in his seat. "Yes. But they don't like the fact that we're a group."

Mindy leaned closer to Warren and whispered, "Do you think they know we're Christians?"

"Probably."

"What's the penalty if we get caught sharing the Gospel?"

"They're pretty tough on Christians. For a long time, they would imprison anyone claiming to be a Christian. They say God doesn't exist. Now they say they have freedom of religion, but I don't think things have changed that much."

"Well, what could they do to us?"

"They'll try to scare us."

"I'm already a little scared," Mindy admitted.

"For Pete's sake, Mindy," Jeff said. "Quit asking so many questions."

They waited in silence for a few minutes.

"Why are they so afraid of Christians?" K.J. finally asked.

"They had a revolution in the late 1950s, and Fidel Castro took over. He brought in Marxism. Karl Marx taught that religion is a lie that keeps people under someone else's power. They believe that anyone promoting Christianity is working against their government. Now the young people are starting to question these beliefs, and the old leaders don't like it. They're afraid of another revolution."

"Yeah. Especially a revolution of love," K.J. said, smiling.

They fell silent again. Jeff passed the time by examining the walls. Every wall was covered with colorful posters of countries around the world. Guam, Switzerland, Germany, Thailand, Egypt, Australia. They were all represented, and many more. Jeff thought it would probably have been easier to go to any of those places than to nearby Cuba.

As if reading his mind, K.J. said, "Boy, would I like to visit some of those places. Where are we going next?"

"Let's just focus on Cuba for now."

Just then, a tall, middle-aged man stood up and motioned for them to come to the back of the room. He directed them to sit in some chairs he had pulled around his desk.

"How does it look?" Warren asked, drawing his chair closer to the desk.

The agent pulled out a file and shook his head. "I'm sorry. They refused your clearance again last night."

"What options do we have left?"

"Since Cuba doesn't have an embassy in the U.S., you have to apply for visas in either Mexico or Canada. The Mexican tour group I'm working with hasn't been able to get approval from their end. You could fly to Mexico City to appeal in person, but I wouldn't recommend that. The only other option is to go from Canada, but you don't have time now."

The kids turned to Warren.

Mindy started sniffling. She looked at Jeff. "I just knew this would happen. You said God would come through. What happened?"

Jeff felt like hitting her. That was Mindy for you. On top of the world one minute and down in the dumps the next.

"Knock it off, Mindy," he said angrily. "You're acting like a spoiled brat."

Warren turned to the agent. "What do you think we should do?"

The agent studied the papers spread out over his desk. "You've paid for the trip to Mexico City. I can refund 80 percent of your money. Then you can try again in a few months."

"We really believe we're supposed to go now," Warren said firmly. "Will you try calling once more?"

"Okay. But the odds are against you."

Warren smiled slightly. "That's nothing new."

"I'll have to wait 20 or 30 minutes until the office in Mexico City opens," the agent said. "Why don't you go to the coffee shop next door and come back in half an hour?"

"We'll wait here," Warren said firmly.

The agent continued, "You know, even if you're cleared, it's pretty risky inside Cuba. Since it's a Communist nation, you won't get much help from our government."

"We can't give up now," Jeff said, running his fingers over the slick poster of Cuba hanging right next to the agent's desk. He was more determined to go than ever.

The group finally agreed to wait in the coffee shop in the next building, keeping an eye on the clock.

The four crowded into a small booth, and Warren entertained Mindy and K.J. with stories about some of his previous trips. He kept them entranced with stories of miraculous conversions and changed lives.

Listening to them talk, Jeff recalled some of the great times he and Warren had had on a couple of "scouting out the land" trips. This was good experience, especially since he wanted to start a video production company when he graduated from college.

Jeff thought he probably inherited his interest in the business from both of his parents. His dad was an anchorman on a local television station, and his mother worked part-time as a news correspondent for the same station.

Jeff's thoughts were interrupted by a roar of laughter. Mindy was back to the subject at hand. "I hope there are showers in Cuba," she said. "I wouldn't want to have to be close to you guys otherwise!"

"By the way," Warren said to her, "fill us in on what you've learned about Cuba." He had assigned her the task of researching the country.

Mindy pulled out her notebook and adjusted her glasses. Then she smiled nervously and reviewed her findings: "Cuba hasn't changed much in over 30 years. Things are pretty old-fashioned there. I think the revolution froze everything in time. It doesn't sound like much construction, renovation, or progress of hardly any kind has taken place."

"Well, I hope they're still driving their cars from the 1950s. I can't wait to see them," K.J. broke in, "and meet some cute Cuban girls."

Jeff didn't laugh. K.J.'s two big interests were cars and girls. And he wasn't sure which K.J. preferred most. It would be hard to keep him focused on their reason for going. He questioned once again the wisdom of including two first-timers on this trip when they didn't know what they might be getting into.

Warren looked at his watch. "We can check back with the travel agent, then we'll have to hurry to make it back to the school on time." As they rose to leave, Warren grabbed K.J.'s arm.

"Wait a minute. I heard something about a problem with the school paper. The principal wants to talk to the person responsible for putting a cartoon in it making fun of him. You wouldn't know anything about that, would you?"

K.J. sighed. "I was hoping you wouldn't ask me that. I was just having a little fun. No harm intended."

"Well, that little joke could just keep you from going on this trip. You'd better watch your step."

Jeff was happy the issue had come up. K.J.'s idea of a joke sometimes got him into trouble. Better to set some ground rules now.

---

The travel agent was just hanging up the phone when they returned.

"I'm sorry. Still no clearance. I had to give them some more information about your reason for going. Somehow they found out you're some kind of religious club."

"Who told them?" Jeff asked, pulling up a chair anxiously.

"They have their ways. But at least they didn't say no. They'll give us an answer in the morning."

"That doesn't give us any time to spare."

"And remember," the agent said, "if your clearance comes through, you'll need to have enough traveler's checks to pay for the flights and Cuban tour package in Mexico City."

The team just looked at K.J.

# Chapter 3

# A Time to Trust

Jeff woke up long before his alarm went off. It was 5:00 a.m., still dark and quiet in the house. Only one day left. *We've cut it too close this time*, he thought.

He tried to control his thoughts. *Lord, where are You? I want to believe You. I thought You wanted us to go to Cuba. Did we hear You wrong?*

He was tired from a restless night. And he was still feeling guilty about not wanting Mindy and K.J. to go on the trip. As a matter of fact, realistically, at this late date it would be impossible to replace either of them.

Somehow he must have dozed off again, because the next thing he knew, he heard an alarm going off and he slapped the button down on his clock. When he reached for the Bible on his nightstand, it fell open to Proverbs 3. The words flew right off the page at him: "Trust in the Lord with all your heart, and lean not on your own understanding."

Bolting straight up in bed, he read on: "In all your ways acknowledge Him, and He shall direct your paths."

He jumped out of bed and repeated the words over and over as he took his shower. "Trust in the Lord. Trust in the Lord. Trust in the Lord."

When Jeff headed downstairs, he took his Bible, still repeating, "Trust in the Lord. Trust in the Lord." He found his dad in the living room reading the morning paper. Mr. Caldwell glanced up and said, "Good morning, Jeff."

Jeff's dad was his hero. Jeff had seen how he held steadfast to his faith through all his problems, big and little.

Jeff's mom came down the stairs with Mindy.

"Mindy says she's going even if she has to hijack the plane," his mom said.

His dad looked up and laughed. "It won't be the first time a plane has been hijacked to Cuba!"

Everyone sat down and Jeff's dad began quizzing him.

"Son, tell me once again what obstacles you're facing with this outreach."

"Before I do, I want to share something I just

read," Jeff said, reaching for his Bible. "This passage of Scripture jumped right out at me this morning."

Everyone listened attentively. "Trust in the Lord with all your heart...."

Mindy looked up in amazement. "So that's what God's up to!"

Jeff told his parents about the problems confronting them: They didn't have the visas to get into Cuba, and K.J. still didn't have the rest of his money. Each of them said a special prayer for the trip, then they headed to the kitchen for breakfast.

The phone rang. Jeff raced to get it, anxious to hear the good news now that he understood God had just been testing them. Mindy was right on his heels.

As Jeff picked up the receiver, everyone gathered around.

"It's Warren," he cupped his hand over the mouthpiece.

Then his face fell. He saw the concern in his family's faces, and turned his back so he could finish the conversation without disappointing them too much.

When Jeff hung up the phone, he said, "Well, you probably know what I'm gonna say already. They still won't clear us."

"Son, can you get in any other way?" his dad asked.

"The only other route is through Canada. But it's too late to try that now."

Mindy smiled. "We'll just have to trust God, won't we?"

Hearing her words, Jeff could almost like her.

Just then, there was a knock on the door. K.J. came strolling in with a huge grin on his face.

"We're on a roll now," he said. "I called the principal and straightened everything out. I apologized for the cartoon, and promised not to do anything like that again. But it's okay. Going on the trip's worth it.

"And what's more, my dad came across! He came over last night and gave me $200. Can you believe that? Is that luck or what?"

"How much do you still need?" Jeff's mother asked.

"Only $250."

"Well," Mindy said, "don't give up yet. Things are just beginning to fall into place."

---

Jeff and K.J. headed straight to the communications department when they got to school. They needed to prepare the equipment for the trip.

They passed Warren coming down the hall, and Jeff stopped him. Jeff noted again how much Warren resembled one of the students. He wasn't much taller than Jeff, wore his sandy brown hair cropped close to his head, and preferred brightly patterned sweaters with slacks to more conservative clothes.

"Have you heard anything?"

"Nothing yet. I've been waiting by the phone."

"Let us know as soon as you hear," Jeff pleaded as he and K.J. headed for the equipment room.

"Even if we don't go, I've seen God working in my life like never before," K.J. said as he cleaned a camera lens.

Jeff frowned. "Hey, stop all this talk about not going. Anyway, what do you mean?"

"Yesterday when you told me you weren't happy about Warren's inviting me to go, I was angry at you."

"It was obvious," Jeff acknowledged.

"But you were right. I wanted to go for the wrong reasons. Just to see the cars and check out the girls. But that's changed."

"In what way?"

K.J. put down the camera he had been working on. "I have a better reason now. I feel like God really wants me to go."

Jeff watched as K.J. reviewed their equipment, making sure everything was ready to go. They were using two of the school's new Canon Hi 8 camcorders. They were small, and the videotapes they used were about the size of a music cassette. But the quality was still excellent.

K.J. also packed the new 3-inch monitor. To review a tape, all you had to do was plug it into a camera and you got color, sound, and a decent picture. They were taking plenty of videotapes and extra battery packs, too.

Suddenly, they were interrupted by a frantic student. "Mr. Russell has a call from Mexico City, and I can't find him anywhere."

"I'll take it," Jeff said, rushing to the phone.

"Can I help you?"

"My name is Mr. Velasquez, and I'm working on a tour for a Mr. Warren Russell."

"I'm Jeff Caldwell. I'm part of his group. Do you know if we've been cleared?"

K.J. crossed his fingers and held his breath.

"You are very lucky, Mr. Caldwell. We have cleared your group to travel. You can pick up your tickets to Cuba tomorrow."

Jeff couldn't believe his ears.

The man went on. "It's rare to get clearance this late. You must know somebody pretty important."

Jeff hung up the phone and grabbed K.J.'s hands. They jumped up and down in a circle, yelling at the top of their voices. "We're going! We're going! We're really going!"

Then suddenly, K.J. stopped.

"Oh, no," he said.

"What's the problem, K.J.?"

"Now I've got to come up with the rest of my money."

# Chapter 4

# Stranger in Mexico City

Jeff couldn't believe he was actually standing at the check-in counter.

And K.J.'s story was even more amazing. K.J. finally got his miracle. Right before his mother left work the day before, her boss asked how the trip plans were going. When she said that K.J. still needed $250, he sat right down and wrote out a check. Not just for the amount of money needed, but for $100 extra. Spending money, he said.

Jeff and Mindy's parents drove the team to the airport. They had been supportive of the idea from the beginning. Now, his mother looked anxiously at Jeff.

"I'm worried about you kids. Please let us know if you run into any trouble."

"Don't worry. Just pray," Jeff said as he looked around for their gate. "Our first test will be this afternoon when we are supposed to pick up our tickets and visas in Mexico."

"God will be with you," Jeff's dad reminded him.

With luggage checked and boarding passes for the flight to Mexico in hand, the team was ready to go at last. K.J. had the job of guarding the equipment.

Jeff was still leery about entrusting K.J. with so much responsibility, but he couldn't handle everything himself. Just managing the team's finances would take a lot of his time.

Mindy was bringing along her laptop computer, a dearly treasured Christmas gift, to record information on everything they filmed. Warren would deal with church leaders, travel agents, tour guides, and hotel personnel.

When the announcement came to board the plane, the team formed a circle with Jeff's parents to pray together one last time. Jeff had never been uncomfortable about praying in public, and Mindy seemed at ease, but Jeff saw K.J. glancing uneasily over his shoulder.

As soon as they had finished, Mindy grabbed her carry-on. "Bye," she yelled and waved. "If we end up in jail, come visit us!" And she disappeared down the tunnel headed for the plane.

The grownups laughed somewhat nervously. Warren shook hands with Jeff and Mindy's parents, thanked them for the ride to the airport, and promised to look after the team.

Cramming all their belongings in the overhead racks and under the seats in front of them, they quickly sat down. K.J. and Mindy had flipped a coin and he had won the window seat on this flight.

Warren and Jeff were in the row behind them. Once in the air, K.J. pulled out his camcorder and began filming fellow passengers.

"You'll have to be careful where you use that thing once we get to Cuba," Jeff warned.

Mindy put her hand over the lens.

"Cool it, Mindy," K.J. said, pushing her away.

"Well, if we get arrested before we even get to Cuba, I'll never forgive you."

Mindy took out her laptop computer and began to peck away at the keys. Jeff had noticed that she always did that when she was bored or apprehensive. He didn't know which it was this time.

While Warren read, Jeff closed his eyes for a few minutes. He must have been more tired than he thought, for amazingly, when he opened them again, the jet was making its final approach into Mexico City.

K.J. pointed his camera to the ground. This was his first trip abroad, and he wanted to film as much as possible. He aimed at some tiny buildings and watched them grow bigger in his viewfinder.

"Boy, even if they stop us here, it would still have been a great trip," he said.

"Don't even think like that," Jeff said. "We're going all the way."

The group gathered all their gear and got off the plane. As soon as they left the airport, the heat and humidity plastered their clothes to their bodies as if they'd just walked through a mild drizzle. Jeff immediately began to look for a place to buy something cold to drink. When he spotted a taco stand right next to a taxi stand, he considered them doubly lucky.

"When does our flight leave Mexico City?" Jeff asked Warren, pulling a handkerchief out of his pocket and mopping his forehead.

"We've got a little over two hours. That should barely give us enough time to get our other tickets and get back here," Warren said.

Warren flagged down a taxi while Jeff paid for the sodas, and they all jumped out of the way as a taxi screeched to a halt at the curb.

Warren handed the driver a brochure with the name and address of the Caribbean Travel Agency on the front in both English and Spanish. Off they went, zigzagging through the most incredible maze of traffic that Jeff had ever seen.

Mindy urged the driver to go even faster, while K.J. tried to identify all the unusual cars he spotted.

The taxi slowed, then stopped in front of a small brown stucco building with "Caribbean Travel Agency" in bold, black letters over the door. Jeff paid the taxi driver, and they got out.

Before they went in, Warren reminded the group, "From now on, we've got to watch everything we say. We don't want to do anything to make the Cuban government change their mind."

Everyone nodded solemnly.

"K.J., put that camcorder away," Mindy urged. "It might be against the rules here or something."

Once inside, they were amazed to hear all the different languages being spoken. Jeff knew some Spanish from a class at school, and he could recognize a little French and Italian. But he was surprised that so many people in the room appeared to be European. Apparently, a lot of people went through Mexico City to get to Cuba.

Warren pulled the team aside. He looked at Mindy and K.J. "You guys wait here. It might be better if only two of us go get the tickets."

"I'm Mr. Russell," he said, approaching the long counter at the back of the room, searching for Mr. Velasquez' nameplate. "We're here to pick up the tickets and vouchers for our Cuban tour." A well-dressed Mexican gentleman glanced up from a stack of papers he was going through.

"Oh, yes, I've been expecting you. You're part of the group we've had all the trouble with. I spoke with a member of your team yesterday."

Jeff spoke up. "I'm the one."

Mr. Velasquez looked at Jeff. "I'm amazed that the authorities changed their minds this late. You must have some good connections."

Jeff and Warren smiled at each other.

As the agent checked their documents, Jeff began to relax a little. They were close now. Nothing could go wrong now, he hoped.

Jeff studied the faces in the crowd. Suddenly, he

noticed a heavyset, middle-aged man leaning against the wall a short distance away. He wore a dark gray suit, with a gray hat low on his forehead. He appeared to be studying a travel brochure, but Jeff was almost sure he had been staring at them.

When the man raised his head slightly, Jeff saw that he had a bushy mustache and heavy eyebrows. The man lowered his eyes quickly when he saw that Jeff had seen him, and pulled the brim of his hat further down.

An uneasy feeling crawled up Jeff's spine, then settled with a chill in his stomach. There was something oddly frightening about the man's face. And those cold, dark eyes. He knew it was no accident that they had been fixed on him.

Jeff elbowed Warren in the ribs and pointed with his head. But when Warren looked where the man had been standing, no one was there. He had vanished into thin air.

Mr. Velasquez shoved their documents across the counter toward Warren.

"Everything's in there. Your hotel and tour vouchers are inside. You'll be met in Havana by your tour guide, a Mr. Franko."

"Our visas aren't in here," Warren said nervously as he thumbed through the packet.

"You'll get them at the Cuban consulate in Merida. We don't issue them here." Jeff leaned his elbow on the counter and sighed. One more hurdle to overcome.

"Where is Merida?" he asked.

"It's a city in the southeastern part of Mexico on the Yucatan Peninsula. Your plane will make a stop there." The agent pointed to it on a large map on the wall behind the counter.

"I'll need the payment for these tour packages, please," the agent said.

Jeff unzipped his money pouch and pulled out a book of traveler's checks. Nervously, he began signing his name. He couldn't shake the feeling that the stranger was still watching him, somewhere out of sight now.

"Warren," he whispered, "is anyone watching us? A big man in a dark gray suit?"

Warren looked around the room. "I don't see anyone matching that description."

"Funny," Jeff shrugged. "How could he disappear so fast?"

As Jeff slid the checks across the counter, Mr. Velasquez said, "Let me warn you about something. Keep your religious activities to yourself. Your group will be closely watched."

Just then, Jeff saw the man again! There was no mistaking it this time. He was standing behind a big potted plant. And he was staring straight at Jeff. Nudging Warren, Jeff looked right at the man. This time Warren saw him, too. This time, the stranger didn't turn away, but stared straight back.

Mr. Velasquez cleared his throat. "One more thing," he said. "Once in Cuba, you'll be on your own. Your government won't be able to help you."

*It seems like I've heard that somewhere before,*

thought Jeff. Only this time, it seemed more ominous.

Jeff and Warren hurried back to the others. K.J. had managed to work his way into a group of young French schoolgirls traveling together, and was trying to speak their language, to the amusement of all. He had dragged Mindy along with him, and she was enjoying herself as much as he was.

Jeff had no patience for all this right now. By the time he extricated them from the group, the stranger had disappeared again.

But somehow, he was sure they would see the man again.

———————

The airport lounge seemed safe enough. With some time on their hands, the group looked over their travel packets carefully. Everything appeared to be in order. For the first time, it seemed that they were really on their way.

Then Jeff felt the hair rise on the back of his neck. He turned quickly and there the man was again! The same big stranger. He was just a few feet away and headed in their direction. He walked right by them and took a seat next to their boarding gate. His eyes seemed to bore into Jeff.

*What nerve!* Jeff thought. He was almost tempted to go right up to the man and ask what he wanted. Then he decided that might not be too wise.

Mindy grabbed Jeff's arm. "Is that the man you were telling us about? He looks scary."

Jeff leaned over to Warren. "What do you think we should do?"

Warren tried to smile. "I'm afraid we'll just have to consider him a new member of our team."

The call went out to board the Cuban Air flight. On board, Jeff helped Mindy and K.J. find their seats. He and Warren were in the row behind them again.

Mindy was in the window seat this time. K.J. smiled as he slid into the middle seat between Mindy and an attractive young girl. Before Jeff and Warren could stash their things away, K.J. had already introduced himself to his seat mate. Jeff overheard her say that her name was Maria, and she was a Cuban returning home from a business trip.

K.J. pulled out his camcorder and began taking pictures of the passengers boarding the plane.

Jeff was worried. He leaned close to Warren. "Do you think that's a good idea?" he said, pointing to K.J.

"Well, I guess it's okay. I see other people doing the same thing. Maybe it's good to let people see us filming a lot. It might look less suspicious later."

"Well, okay, Warren. But you gotta keep an eye on him. He's such a cut-up. Sometimes he just gets carried away."

"Don't worry, Jeff. This is all new to him. He'll settle down."

Jeff saw the mysterious stranger coming down the aisle. He leaned forward and whispered hoarsely to K.J., "That's him! Try to get his picture."

K.J. kept his camcorder running as the stranger came down the aisle. The man kept walking to the back of the plane. Jeff shuddered. He had never seen anyone so intimidating. He didn't like the idea that the man was sitting behind them where he could see everything they did.

"Did you get him?" Jeff asked.

"Yeah. I got some great shots of him," K.J. said. "They just might come in handy."

When the plane took off, there was nothing for Jeff to do but sit back and enjoy the ride. For the first time, he noticed the man sitting next to him, by the window.

The man had a round face and sparse salt and pepper hair that began at the top of a very high forehead. His stomach almost hid his seat belt. When he smiled and extended his hand to Jeff, it was obvious that his nails were bitten on a regular basis.

Jeff smiled back and shook the man's hand. He reminded Jeff of his grandfather.

"My name is Mr. Sanchez," he said. "I see that you're traveling with friends."

"I'm Jeff Caldwell. And this is Warren Russell, my teacher. My sister and a friend are in the row in front of us."

Mr. Sanchez turned out to be quite a talker. He filled Jeff and Warren in on his background. He was a native of Cuba, a high-ranking government official, in fact, just returning from a trip to Mexico. Jeff learned a great many things about Cuba that Mindy's research hadn't turned up – mainly about the Cuban people.

It wasn't long before Jeff found himself telling Mr. Sanchez a little about the Reel Kids club. Mr. Sanchez listened with great interest. Jeff began to wonder what he found so interesting. He wondered if it were an accident that they had been seated next to each other.

Mr. Sanchez couldn't seem to hear enough about Jeff. He asked about his family, school, and hobbies. And he asked lots of questions about the Reel Kids. But Jeff sensed that there was something else Mr. Sanchez wanted to talk about. He just didn't know how yet.

Before long, they were directly over the Meridian peninsula. High blue waves splashed against the rocky shores below them. Lit up in the bright afternoon sun, the waves were almost the same color as the sky. The announcement came on to tighten their seat belts.

Jeff still couldn't forget the look in the mysterious stranger's eyes. He was sure the man was assigned to watch them. Then a painful thought occurred to Jeff: What if Mr. Sanchez were also there to watch them? Maybe if the stranger couldn't get close enough to them to do whatever his job was, this friendly seat mate could.

Then the whining noise of the jets gave way to the screeching of tires, and the plane bumped along the runway. A flight attendant announced, "We will be on the ground in Merida for 90 minutes. Please take all valuables with you as you leave. We cannot be responsible for anything left on the plane." Jeff patted his waist to make sure his money pouch was still safely tied around it.

The attendant continued, "Please return to your same seat when reboarding."

Jeff leaned over to Warren and whispered, "That's good. I'll be able to talk to Mr. Sanchez some more during the flight to Cuba. I want to find out why he's so friendly. I've got a feeling there's some unfinished business there.

# Chapter 5

# Merida

Did you notice how friendly Mr. Sanchez was?" Jeff mentioned again to Warren in the Meridian airport. "Why do you think that is?" Jeff slung his black bag over his shoulder.

"I don't think it's an accident that he's sitting next to us. I don't know why, but I have a feeling we'll find out before we land in Cuba."

Mindy couldn't hold back her excitement. "K.J. met a girl named Maria. He talked to her the whole way. I heard her say that she was raised Catholic, and she seems to know a lot about the Bible."

"I was just being friendly," K.J. protested.

Mindy moved closer to Jeff so she wouldn't have to talk too loudly. "I felt real bad when she told me how her family feels about God now. All of them except for Maria have rejected Him."

K.J. smiled. "I offered to pray with her."

Spotting the Cuban consulate office, Jeff gasped at the length of the line.

"Oh, man! It'll be a miracle if we get through before the plane leaves!"

They took their place at the back of the line and waited as patiently as possible while an official walked up and down checking passports. When he got closer to the Reel Kids, Warren drew the team around him.

"Now be careful. Let's go over our purpose for the trip one more time so nobody messes up. We're doing a study on Cuba's history and culture. We're making a video to take back to our high school. It's for educational purposes. Okay?"

When Jeff was finally at the front of the line, he surrendered his travel documents to a stern official.

"I see you're an American."

"Yes, sir."

He looked through the documents. "I understand you are traveling with some other Americans."

"That's right."

The official lowered Jeff's documents and glared directly into his eyes. "We've been waiting for you. You and your friends are to come with me."

Jeff thought his heart would pound out of his chest. He turned to stare at the ashen faces of his friends. They followed the officer single file into a small office.

Jeff dared not look at Mindy. He knew she'd burst into tears if he did.

Another official walked in. "All of you be seated."

"What seems to be the problem?" Warren asked. He tried to keep his voice calm. "I thought we had been cleared."

The official glared at him. "Sit down, I said. We understand you are some kind of religious group."

Nobody breathed.

"What exactly are your plans?" the official asked as he scrutinized them one by one.

"We're part of a Christian communications club," Warren said. "Our purpose in going to Cuba is to study the country and visit some of its churches."

The official wrinkled his forehead. "I've been told by our office in Cuba to issue you a warning. You are not to stir up our people with your American ideas."

"Christianity is not just an American idea," Warren ventured bravely.

"Be that as it may. I warn you: You can be put in jail for spreading your beliefs in our country."

"We were told it's okay to share in the churches," Warren stood his ground.

"Only in the churches. And you can only give a personal testimonial."

"Then that's what we'll do," Warren promised.

Jeff could hear loud voices in the hall. Some sort of heated discussion was going on. Leaning forward to look through the doorway, Jeff could just barely make out that it was Mr. Sanchez and a man in a uniform. The man's jacket was covered with ribbons and medals, so Jeff figured that he must be pretty important.

*That settles it,* Jeff thought. He was a fool to have trusted Mr. Sanchez. He was a fool to have told him about the Reel Kids. Mr. Sanchez must have turned them in. Whatever happened now, it would all be Jeff's fault.

The official who had been questioning them heard the commotion, too. He stopped talking and walked out into the hall. Jeff sneaked up to the door to get a better look at what was going on. Mr. Sanchez pointed his finger at their interrogator and practically screamed at him.

Then the group in the hallway broke up. Jeff scurried back to his chair just as the official walked in.

"You can pick up your visas at the window," he said almost angrily.

Jeff was astonished. He looked at the others. Mindy's eyes were as big as saucers. So were K.J.'s. And even Warren's.

Mindy was fearless now. She jumped out of her chair. "Well, it's about time!"

"Just pick up your visas before I change my mind."

After picking up their visas, the group went to the boarding area. As soon as the call came to reboard the plane, they were among the first to their seats. They couldn't wait to see the last of Merida.

K.J.'s new friend, Maria, was already seated. She

turned to K.J. and asked, "Why were they giving you such a hard time in there?"

K.J. shrugged. He didn't know whom to trust now.

When Mr. Sanchez came down the aisle, Jeff stood up to let him slide by. Warren was in the back waiting to use the bathroom.

"Thanks for helping us," Jeff ventured, watching closely for his reaction.

"You're welcome," Mr. Sanchez said and smiled warmly. "I'm sorry for the way you were treated. They're afraid of your views about God. I'm not. I haven't always been a Communist, you know. I was born into a religious family."

"Really?" Jeff asked. "What happened?"

"After the revolution, I rejected my belief in God and became a Communist."

Jeff couldn't believe his ears. He was talking to a Cuban leader who was a Communist, but freely admitted to a past belief in God. Now he knew it was no accident that they were seated together.

Jeff said a quick, silent prayer. *Lord*, he prayed, *I don't think You sent me on this trip just to speak at churches. I think You want me to talk to this man.*

"What was there about communism that attracted you?" Jeff asked.

"At first, I thought I had found the missing piece of the puzzle. The puzzle of life," Mr. Sanchez said.

"And?"

"Not just me, but everybody thought that communism was the answer to all our problems."

"And?"

"Now I have my doubts."

"But you're a leader. What did you do in the revolution?"

"I was asked by Mr. Castro to bring about some important changes in my country. I trusted him; he seemed like a good man. The hope of the people.

"In the beginning, we were a model nation. Now I've seen too many promises broken."

"Such as?"

"The promise of freedom, for one. Cuba is in an economic crisis. The Soviets have abandoned us for democracy."

Mr. Sanchez described how during the revolution, the Communists took over the work force, the schools, and the communications systems. Anyone thought to be resistant to the changes was thrown into prison, even if they had been friends of those ordering their arrests. In short, anyone who got in their way was arrested.

"Is it still the same?" Jeff ventured.

"The leaders keep tight control of everything. Nothing gets past them."

"I have a feeling that you have some doubts about God now," Jeff said bravely. "Am I right?"

"I'm not sure what to believe. I know there's more to religion than what I experienced as a child. I wasn't satisfied with the things I was taught. I didn't like the cold formality. I didn't like the impersonalness. So that discontent left me open to other ideas."

Jeff shared his own story with Mr. Sanchez. He

told how he, too, had a lot of doubts as a child. He also told about his later decision to accept Jesus Christ as his personal Savior.

He knew Warren was listening, standing just a few rows behind them in the aisle. He felt certain that Warren knew what was going on, and was praying for him. Then Jeff reached into his sports bag and took out his Bible.

"Would you let me share some words from the Bible with you?" he asked.

Mr. Sanchez nodded his head. He listened intently as Jeff shared some of his favorite Scriptures.

"How can anyone know for sure that there is a God?" Mr. Sanchez almost pleaded.

Jeff knew this was his opening. He told Mr. Sanchez about a car accident he'd had. A brush with death at the age of nine.

"The doctors had given up on me. But God saved me. God gave me a new life in Him."

"You're lucky. Nothing that dramatic has ever happened to me."

"It doesn't have to take a dramatic event. My parents told me about Jesus, of course, from the time I was born. But it was only a bunch of stories to me. It meant nothing until I experienced Him myself."

He saw a strange look in Mr. Sanchez' eyes.

"Mr. Sanchez," he dared. "Would you like to know Jesus?"

"Yes. But how?" He reached for a handkerchief.

Jeff paused only a moment. He knew the Spirit of the Lord was opening this man's heart. He couldn't let this opportunity pass.

"By inviting Jesus into your heart. You can do it with a simple prayer."

"We must be careful that no one sees us," Mr. Sanchez warned. "It could be very bad for both of us."

Jeff turned around to make sure no one was watching. He noticed that the mysterious stranger's seat was empty. The cabin lights were dimmed. They seemed safe enough.

He leaned closer to Mr. Sanchez. "We'll pray with our eyes open. No one will know except God."

"But how will I know what to pray? It's been so long," Mr. Sanchez asked.

"I'll help you. The most important thing is that you mean what you say. Just repeat after me: 'Jesus, come into my heart and be my Lord.'" Mr. Sanchez repeated the words.

After they had finished, Warren quietly slipped back into his seat. He handed Jeff some literature from his carry-on to give to Mr. Sanchez to help him grow in the Lord.

Then Jeff saw the stranger standing in the aisle just a few rows ahead of them. How long had he been standing there? The man brushed Warren's arm as he hurried to the back of the plane. He appeared to be upset about something.

Jeff elbowed Mr. Sanchez. "Do you know him?"

"Oh, yes. I've seen him before. He's part of the Cuban secret police."

"What does that mean?"

"'They're like the KGB.'"

"I've heard bad stories about the KGB. Do they do the same things?" Jeff asked anxiously.

"They're all trained the same way. They always have someone on these flights. I'd say it looks like this guy has been assigned to your group."

"Then you saw the way he looked at us?"

"It's his job to intimidate you."

"Well, he's sure doing a good job."

The tension was broken when they noticed K.J. in the aisle with his camcorder going, filming the few passengers who weren't dozing. Mindy was next to him with her notebook, attempting to interview the passengers as K.J. filmed them. Thankfully, the ones they had chosen were being cooperative.

Just then, the captain came on the intercom to announce that they were only 75 miles outside Havana. The cabin lights came on.

As the captain was speaking, the plane began to shake. Mindy fell right into the lap of the lady she was talking to. K.J. grabbed the arm of a seat to steady himself, and lowered his camera.

The plane shook more violently, and the passengers could hear a steady whining. A flight attendant's voice came on the intercom, urging everyone to return to their seats immediately and fasten their seat belts. The passengers were starting to panic.

The steady whining gave way to a thunderous roar. Jeff could feel the floor vibrating wildly. He looked at Warren and Mr. Sanchez, then all three stared straight ahead, unable to speak.

Finally, Mr. Sanchez blurted out, "Something is

wrong. Terribly wrong!"

Mindy lifted herself off her seat enough to turn around and stare at Jeff. Her face was as white as her shirt. "What's wrong, Jeff?" she begged. "Are we gonna crash?"

Jeff couldn't answer her. He had no answer. By now, the plane was circling the Havana airport, still shaking violently.

Warren grabbed Jeff's hand. "This is definitely an attack from the enemy! We must pray. And fast.

"In Jesus' name, we take authority over the enemy..." Warren began. He repeated it twice.

Almost immediately, the noise stopped. The plane stopped vibrating. The passengers fell silent and waited expectantly.

"Man, that was close!" Jeff said.

"I have a feeling we're going to have to stay on guard this whole trip," Warren cautioned.

Through Mr. Sanchez' window, Jeff could see tiny lights begin to shimmer against the dark background below. He let out a nervous laugh and tightened his seat belt in preparation for landing. He turned to the Cuban beside him.

"Mr. Sanchez, do you think your nation is ready for a different kind of revolution?"

"It's only a matter of time."

*Maybe sooner than you think,* Jeff thought.

# Chapter 6

# Questioned

The Reel Kids were finally in Cuba! In the airport terminal, Jeff shook his new friend's hand. "Mr. Sanchez, I'll never forget this day."

"Nor I. Here's my address and phone number. If you need anything, please call me."

While the group waited for their luggage, Jeff pointed out to Warren a man standing on a bench. He had a long black mustache and shiny, straight black hair which he covered with a pink straw hat. He wore a shirt with huge pink, purple, and red blossoms on it, and he waved a long stick with a white sign nailed to the top. The sign was marked Franko Tours.

Warren walked over to him.

"My name is Warren Russell, and I believe we are in your tour group."

"Yes," he said, checking off their names. "You're the last to arrive. The others are waiting on the bus. Please get your luggage and go through immigration as quickly as you can. It's been a long day."

Warren walked back to the baggage carousel. Mindy clutched her laptop and tried out some Spanish phrases on two girls who were also waiting for their luggage. K.J. leaned against a post, talking with Maria and writing something on a piece of paper.

When all their luggage was stacked together, Jeff noticed something was missing. He glanced at K.J.

"K.J., where's the camera bag?"

"Oh no! I don't believe it. I left it on the plane!" And he took off running.

Jeff kicked the floor. They had given K.J. only one job to do, and he'd already blown it.

When K.J. returned, the camera bag was over his shoulder, and he was beaming an embarrassed grin. The grin disappeared when he realized that Maria had left.

"Sorry," he said. "There was a lot going on right before we landed."

"Don't worry about it," Mindy said. "I found some people I could practice my Spanish on."

"We need to hurry," Warren said. "After such a tiring day, I imagine everyone is ready for bed. Especially the other people in our tour group. I don't know how long they've been waiting."

They headed toward the immigration area when K.J. stopped dead still. "Hey, I don't believe it. There's that guy again," he said. "What do you make of it?"

"I already know who he is," Jeff replied. "I'll fill you in later."

"Look. He's coming our way. And he's got some kind of armed guard with him. What should we do?" Mindy cried.

"Just keep walking," Warren said. "Don't stop."

But the men walked up and blocked their path.

"All of you, come with us."

"What do we do now?" Mindy whispered.

"I think we'd better do what they say," Warren whispered back.

They followed the men into an office walled halfway down with glass.

"Wait here. We'll be right back," the guard said as he and the stranger left the room.

Mindy started to cry. This confirmed it. Jeff knew they shouldn't have brought her. Or K.J. He had been right all along. They couldn't take the pressure. But she was his sister, and he had promised his parents that he would look out for her. He walked over and put his arm around her.

"Are you all right?"

"I'm scared. Aren't you?"

Warren reached for Mindy's hand. "We haven't done anything wrong. They can't do anything to us."

The two men returned shortly. The uniformed man closed the door.

"I'm with immigration here in Havana," he said. "This is Mr. Garcia. He's with our secret police. He tells me you were trying to coerce one of our high government officials on the plane."

Jeff was astonished at the hatred he saw in Mr. Garcia's eyes.

"Mr. Garcia is lying. He knows we haven't done anything wrong." Jeff couldn't contain himself.

Mr. Garcia raised his hand as if to strike Jeff.

Warren stepped between them.

"Then why did you appear to be praying with him?" Mr. Garcia asked.

"Since when is it a crime to pray?" Warren asked.

"We have strict rules about Christian activities in public," Mr. Garcia said.

"We were on an airplane in free airspace," K.J. interjected.

"It was a Cuban plane with Cubans on board. You were warned not to share your religious ideas, weren't you?" Mr. Garcia demanded.

"Yes," Jeff said. "But I was just answering some questions for him. I had to answer them honestly."

Mr. Garcia's face filled with rage. "I've been watching all of you since Mexico City. That one," he said, pointing to K.J., "even took my picture on the plane. You could all be put in jail for that."

"Did you know the man sitting next to you?" the immigration official asked Jeff.

"Not until we met on the plane. He told me he works for the Cuban government."

"What else did he tell you?" Mr. Garcia snapped.

"He told me about the changes that have taken place in your country in the last 30 years."

Mr. Garcia turned his gaze to K.J. "And what about the girl sitting next to you. She also is a Cuban citizen. What did she tell you?"

"She didn't say much," K.J. defended. "I just like talking to girls."

Now the official turned to Mindy. "And what did she say to you?"

"We discussed our countries. She asked me why I acted so happy all the time."

"And what was your answer?"

"I told her about the most important thing in my life. I told her about my relationship with God."

There was complete silence in the room. For the first time in a long time, Jeff was really proud of Mindy. She had merely told the truth. He spoke up, "Sir, many other people would say the same thing. I don't think that's a crime."

Mr. Garcia ignored him. "Show us your passports." The group handed over their passports.

"Your luggage is being brought here. We're going to search it for any propaganda you might have with you. It will go easier for you if you tell us now if you're carrying something illegal."

"We have some Bibles. Nothing unusual," Warren said.

"Is that all?" Mr. Garcia asked.

"Some gifts for people we might meet."

"And what about this camera equipment?" Mr. Garcia was rummaging through the camera bag.

"We do reports on foreign countries and take them back to our high school," Warren said. "That way our students can learn about other places."

K.J. reached for his camcorder defiantly. "I saw lots of other people with camcorders on the plane."

They were interrupted by porters carrying in their luggage, piling it in the middle of the room. Mr. Garcia walked over to the suitcases. "Open these, please."

Jeff was the first to unzip his suitcase.

Mr. Garcia reached inside Jeff's bag and pulled out a package of New Testaments. "Are these the gifts you were talking about?"

"Yes, that's right," Warren spoke up.

Mr. Garcia turned next to Mindy's suitcase and motioned for her to open it. He pulled a box of New Testaments out of her suitcase. "And I assume these are gifts, too?"

She nodded.

Then he noticed some religious tracts stuck in the corner of her bag. He tossed them on the floor angrily. Then he shook his head and sat down in a chair.

"Do you know what kind of trouble you could have gotten in if you were caught with this later?"

"We heard you have freedom of religion now," Warren said.

The students held their breath.

The room was silent for what seemed like an eternity.

"Our nation is one of the most progressive in the world. Our government protects our people from faulty ideas," Mr. Garcia explained calmly.

Mindy's face turned red. "Are you saying my love for God is a bad idea?"

"Believing in God is a foreign idea to us," Mr. Garcia said. "It does our people no good." He threw a Bible on the floor. "Maybe this God is good for you. But not for us!"

There was silence again. They had been in the room almost half an hour. *The rest of our tour group must really be boiling by now,* Jeff thought.

Mr. Garcia turned to Warren. "Would you like us to arrest you now? Or would you rather have us put you on the next plane back to Mexico City?"

"Neither," he said. "We would like to see your country. We will try to observe your laws."

Mr. Garcia crossed the room and conferred with the other official. When he turned around, he said, "We'll let you stay. But keep your ideas to yourself. Next time you won't be so lucky."

# Chapter 7

# New Friends

They already knew that they weren't going to make the tour guide's list of favorite people. Hostile, sweaty, and tired, the other members of their tour group were waiting impatiently when they got to the bus. Mr. Franko shook his head and exclaimed, "Well, it's about time!"

One passenger muttered in disgust, "Here come the drug dealers."

No one on the team bothered to explain. They took their seats as quickly as they could. "Don't say anything," Warren warned. "They'll forget about it after a good night's sleep."

K.J. checked out the bumpy roads that led to their hotel. "Look at that car!" he exclaimed, punching Mindy. "How old do you think it is?"

"I have no idea. And I don't care. I'm just looking forward to a nice, soft bed to go to sleep in. Why are you so interested in cars, anyway?"

"Oh, I don't know. Maybe because my dad's a mechanic."

"Hey, look at those cute girls," Mindy teased him, pointing to a group of girls gathered outside a market. "That should interest you more than cars."

Jeff noticed that although it was quite late, the streets were filled with children. They darted in and out of the traffic and played in groups along the sides of the road. The buildings they passed appeared to be very old, in need of a good facelift. Many were laced with scaffolding.

The bus pulled up to the Riviera Hotel, nestled in the midst of palm trees. Soft winds rustled the palms, and moonlight lit a beach behind the hotel.

Tall, round cement columns lined the front of the hotel and supported a balcony above the entrance. Fancy wrought iron covered the windows to the rooms. Jeff was happy to note that it looked just the way the brochure had described it.

When the bus finally ground to a stop, Jeff checked his watch. He couldn't believe it was almost ten. *I must be running on adrenaline,* he thought.

As they stepped off the bus, it was obvious that the hotel had undergone considerable restoration. Globs of fallen plaster were lying on the ground around the building. Jeff walked over to one of the gigantic columns and ran his hand over its rough surface.

Though weathered by time, the hotel was still stately and beautiful. Strategically placed potted trees helped disguise the disrepair.

The lobby was spacious, with high ceilings and a tiled floor. Gigantic murals of past heroes and living legends lined the walls along with smaller gilt-framed landscapes. A portrait of Fidel Castro overshadowed them all. Jeff forgot the hassles of the day in his excitement of actually being there.

With a scowl on his face, Mr. Franko gathered the team together and they braced themselves for a tongue lashing.

"I've already gone over all this with the others while we were waiting for you. You won't get into any more trouble if you follow my instructions."

Mr. Franko handed each of them a sheet of yellow paper. "Here's the schedule. Read it carefully."

"When do we go to the beach?" K.J. asked.

"It's on the schedule, kid."

Jeff saw on the schedule that two beach trips were planned: one on Monday and one on Tuesday. That should make K.J. happy.

Mr. Franko handed Warren another piece of paper. "This explains the currency exchange system. You can use U.S. dollars in the tourist shops, but you need Cuban pesos for the local markets and stores."

Warren handed the currency guide to Jeff. Mindy and K.J. continued to study the activity schedule.

"Any questions?" Mr. Franko asked as he looked at his watch.

"When's our free time?" Mindy asked.

"Tomorrow. It's Sunday. I'll see you first thing Monday morning. Bright and early. Be on time. And please pay close attention to the rules and regulations on the back of your itinerary. Don't forget, you're in a Communist country."

When Mr. Franko was safely out of sight, a distinguished man in a dark blue suit approached them. He stuck out his hand to Warren. "I'm Mr. Ward. I've been on all your flights since Los Angeles. What happened back there at the airport?"

Warren moved a step closer to the man and lowered his voice. "We got in a little trouble talking with one of their officials on the plane. No big deal."

"Well," Mr. Ward offered, "I come here on business a lot. This is a short trip for me this time. I'm taking the first flight back Monday morning, but if you need any help before that, let me know."

"By the way," Mr. Ward said, turning to Jeff, "forgive me for staring at you. But you look so familiar. Have we met before?"

Jeff knew what the problem was and grinned. "My name's Jeff Caldwell. You've probably seen my father. He's an anchorman on a TV station in Los Angeles. Everyone tells us we look exactly alike."

"That's it. I watch him all the time."

With that, they shook hands and parted. But when Mr. Ward turned toward the elevators, Warren glimpsed something that looked like the corner of a

Bible sticking out of the side pocket of his carry-on. He was almost positive that was what it was.

Then Jeff and Warren made their way over to the registration desk. Jeff couldn't wait to get to his room and take a cool shower. Mindy sat lifeless on her suitcase. It was obvious that she was done for the day.

K.J. was lounging in a big overstuffed chair, one leg draped over the side, his eyes riveted on their bags. He wasn't about to let the cameras out of his sight again. He didn't look like he had much energy, either.

A young couple holding Russian passports were the only ones ahead of them waiting to register. They turned and smiled at Warren and Jeff as they waited for the desk clerk to verify their reservation.

"We saw you at the airport," the young woman said in broken English. "You must be very important people. So many men in uniforms around you."

Jeff and Warren smiled and shrugged, but offered no explanation.

"I'd love to visit your country some day," she went on. "And you should come to ours."

Jeff thought about what she had just said. They had just been invited to visit the nation that had once so tightly controlled all of Cuba's affairs. The whole world was really in transition now.

When Warren signed the registration book, the clerk handed him keys to two rooms. "Here you are, sir. Rooms 626 and 627."

K.J. and Mindy joined them in the elevator, and K.J. perked up. "The sixth floor? That's great. I can get some good street shots out the window."

Their rooms looked very comfortable. The larger room had a double bed and two single beds with matching green and brown plaid bedspreads. A window overlooked the street, just as K.J. had hoped, and was draped with a long plaid curtain matching the bedspreads. Two green chairs faced each other by a small table in front of the window. The dark brown carpet, though spotted by time and wear, was still presentable. And they were glad to see an adjoining bathroom with a shower.

The room next door had twin beds covered with faded blue bedspreads. There was a small desk and chair in the corner. Faded blue curtains completed the decorations. That room also had a private bath.

It was quickly decided that the men would share the larger room and give the other to Mindy.

Warren said, "I know it's late, but I think we need to thank God for His protection so far." They gathered in the larger room, all sitting on the double bed, and each of them lifted up a short prayer. Then Warren pulled out the tour schedule.

"Tomorrow's a free day. You're scheduled to share at a church tomorrow morning. The church youth leader will meet you here tomorrow morning at 8:00. His name is Emmanuel. He'll tell you how to get there. Now Jeff, since you've been on several trips with me before, I'm putting you in charge for the day. Make sure you watch out for K.J. and Mindy. I'm counting on you."

"Where will you be?" K.J. asked.

"I'll be meeting with the man who's arranging our schedule for the rest of the week."

Mindy looked nervous. "Do you think we should still go to that church after what happened today?"

"It's not against the law to go to church. They're just trying to scare us."

"Are you sure we're supposed to speak tomorrow? We just got here." K.J. said tiredly.

"You'll be okay after a night's rest. Just share your conversion stories. But be careful. Someone from the secret police will probably be there."

The discussion ended. Jeff walked Mindy to her room, looking to make sure it was empty. Then he left, knowing she'd be sound asleep in no time.

Once he got in bed, Jeff couldn't fall asleep. He couldn't turn his mind off. He was worried about Mr. Sanchez. Being such a new Christian, would he be able to handle the pressure he was sure to come under?

He lay on his back for hours with his eyes closed, trying every trick he knew to fall asleep. But he kept imagining the faces of all the people Mr. Sanchez had told him about. Those who were homeless because of the wrecked economy, the ones imprisoned for their political beliefs, the ones who wanted to stay true to their faith but were too afraid to resist. Finally, Jeff's fatigue prevailed and he fell into a restless sleep.

---

The sun was shining through the window when Jeff opened his eyes. Warren was already dressed.

Jeff sat up. "Warren, can I ask you a question?"

"Sure, Jeff. Shoot."

"Why is Satan allowed to control so much of the world?"

Warren turned to Jeff. "Satan is our enemy, and would lack the power to control so much if the Church did their job. Cuba can be freed through prayer and enough people willing to come here to help."

That statement sobered Jeff. They weren't here to play games.

He walked to the window and yelled for K.J. to get up. The streets were already noisy and bustling with people. Jeff was anxious to get out there with them. He showered quickly, then opened his Bible to prepare his heart for the Sunday gathering.

K.J. was just coming out of the bathroom when Warren started to leave. "I know you guys will do a great job. I have faith in you. Just be careful."

"When do you think you'll get back?" Jeff asked.

"Late afternoon. We're supposed to meet some church leaders. I should get back about the same time as you. I'll see you tonight."

Jeff knocked on the wall, and in a few minutes Mindy joined them to rehearse what each of them would say. A knock on the door interrupted them.

Jeff opened the door to an immaculately dressed young Cuban about the same size as he was. When the young man smiled, Jeff noticed Mindy staring enviously at his perfect, evenly matched white teeth.

"My name is Emmanuel. Are you the Reel Kids?"

"That's us. Please come in," Jeff said. "I'm Jeff, this is my friend, K.J., and my sister, Mindy."

"We're glad you're here. Here's a map to our church. It's best if we go there separately. Please be careful; you're probably being watched."

"How did you ever guess?" K.J. asked jokingly.

"I heard about what happened at the airport. News gets around."

"If we speak at your church, will they arrest us?" Mindy asked.

"Not just for sharing your testimony. Only if you try to stir up the people to action."

Emmanuel looked at his watch. "I've got to leave now. Follow these directions and I'll see you in a little while."

After saying goodbye, the team studied the map.

They carefully followed the route Emmanuel had marked, beginning at the hotel. It took them down what appeared to be one of the main streets of Havana. Jeff held the folded map in front of him, close to his body.

After they had been walking a few minutes, he said, "Turn right here. We go about six more blocks and then turn left. Then another right and we should be able to see the church."

While they were walking, Jeff spotted a number of soldiers with rifles over their shoulders. For the first time, he realized how controlled Cuba really was.

They were so intent on following Emmanuel's directions that when they looked up, they were standing right in front of the church.

Jeff hurried the team inside. A handful of people sat in clusters of chairs around the room. They were dressed in simple, everyday clothes. Jeff noticed that the room was very small, with no pews, ornate altar, or stained glass windows. No microphones, either.

He looked for Emmanuel, and jumped when he felt a hand touch his shoulder.

"Congratulations. You made it," Emmanuel said.

"You sound surprised."

"I'll be translating for you this morning," Emmanuel said. "Just say one sentence at a time, then I'll translate it into Spanish. Be sure to tell the others."

Emmanuel took Jeff aside. "There are two men here I've never seen before." He pointed them out.

"Secret police?"

"Probably."

A small Cuban woman began to play the piano softly, and two men accompanied her on guitars. The people joined them in singing songs of their faith.

Jeff took a seat between Mindy and K.J. Emmanuel went to stand behind an old wooden pulpit.

"We're glad to have special guests from America here today. They call themselves the Reel Kids. Let's welcome their leader, Jeff Caldwell."

When Emmanuel introduced the team to the people in the room, he spoke first in Spanish and then in English. It dawned on Jeff that hardly anyone there spoke English. No wonder Emmanuel had volunteered to interpret for them.

When Jeff approached the pulpit, K.J. pulled out his camcorder and began filming. Jeff glanced at the two strangers to see if they would object.

"I'm happy to be here today. I want to share...." Jeff tried to concentrate on his words. He had just begun speaking when there was a rustle in the room. Chairs slid across the wooden floor with a loud scratching sound. The two strangers stood up. They walked over to K.J. One of them leaned down and whispered something to him.

K.J. immediately tucked the camcorder back into his bag. Mindy ducked her head and stared at the floor. Then the two men returned to their seats.

Jeff continued with his story. He told about his car accident, and how God had spared his life. He told how he had accepted the Son of God to be his Savior. Emmanuel related the story right along with him.

Jeff could see that his story was touching some of those listening. Tears flowed freely down the cheeks of two older women on the front row. Others dabbed at their eyes or nodded.

The two men were standing in the back of the room now. Jeff decided it was time to introduce Mindy.

Mindy bravely stood up and marched right up to the pulpit. It was her first time to do anything like this, but she didn't flinch or waver. She confidently told how God had come to be real in her life. Then K.J. followed. His message was less polished, but no less significant. Not a sound was heard while they spoke.

Jeff had never spoken to people who were so eager to hear what he had to say. After they finished, Emmanuel invited everyone to come forward to pray for the team. The people gathered around and bowed their heads as Emmanuel prayed. When Jeff raised his head again, he noticed that the doors of the church were just closing. The two men had left.

After the service, the team joined the congregation at a special Cuban lunch of chicken baked in a green chile sauce. It was served with spicy black beans and crusty bread. Some of the women in the church had prepared the meal.

The afternoon was spent answering questions and playing Cuban games. Emmanuel gave them an extensive tour of the neighborhood.

Finally, Emmanuel looked at his watch. "It's almost 5:30. You should go back to your hotel now."

Walking back to the hotel was the first chance they'd had to be alone. "I'm glad that's over," Mindy said. "I've never done anything like that before."

Jeff turned to K.J. "What did that guy tell you?"

"Just to put my camcorder away. He said it's illegal to film in a church."

"K.J., I'm tired of your getting us in trouble," Mindy snapped.

"That's my job," K.J. responded with a grin.

"What? To get us in trouble?"

"Drop it, you two," Jeff said. "We're all tired. Let's just concentrate on getting back to the hotel."

----

As soon as they got off the elevator, they saw a package wrapped in plain brown paper lying in front of Mindy's door. She ran and picked it up.

"Careful," K.J. kidded. "Maybe it's a bomb."

"Yeah, pretty funny, K.J.," Mindy said. But she carefully set it back on the floor.

# Chapter 8

# A Desperate Decision

Jeff watched as Mindy unlocked her door and K.J. slid the package into her room with his foot. They circled it and examined it carefully. There wasn't a clue what was in it or where it came from.

Mindy's curiosity finally got the better of her. "Move back," she said bravely.

Ripping away the paper, she lifted the lid on a cardboard box. The guys gathered around. Jeff couldn't believe what he saw. The box was filled with pieces of beautiful old china. Cups. Saucers. Plates. Vases. Even a teapot. Mindy pulled out the fragile items one by one.

Jeff spotted an envelope in the bottom of the box.

Mindy beat him to it. She pulled a card out of the envelope and held it against her chest. "It was to me. I'm gonna read it first."

She hunched over the card so the guys couldn't see. "Guess what? It's from Mr. Sanchez!"

Mindy handed the card to Jeff. Then she picked up some of the china and held it up to the light so she could read what was written on the bottom.

Jeff read the note, then said, "Mr. Sanchez says hello to everybody. He sends us his thanks. He says he's never known peace like he knows now. He's sorry about the trouble we had at the airport. He says that they questioned him, too."

"I hope he didn't get in trouble," Mindy said.

Jeff turned the card over. "He says he's deeply grateful that he met us."

Mindy held a teacup out to Jeff. "This stuff is real expensive. Mom and I saw some like it in a big fancy store one time. I bet it's been in his family a long time."

Mindy looked at her watch. "It's 6:30 now. I wonder why Warren's not back. And I wonder when Mr. Sanchez came by here."

K.J. walked to the window and looked down at the street. He cried out, "Hey, you guys! Some soldiers have a prisoner!"

Jeff and Mindy ran over to see for themselves. Four armed soldiers surrounded a man right under their window. Then two more soldiers came. A large man in a gray suit and hat joined the group.

As they looked closer, the prisoner glanced up at

their room. They gasped in unison as they recognized his round face and balding head. K.J. mouthed the words for them all: "They've got Mr. Sanchez!"

K.J. ran to get his camcorder. He screwed on the zoom lens and adjusted it quickly. He leaned out the window and looked through it. "I can see them better now. Oh no! Mr. Garcia is the guy in the gray suit!"

Jeff grabbed the camera from K.J.'s hands and looked through it. He aimed it right at Mr. Sanchez' face.

"Uh oh. He looks like he's in big trouble. Now I'm sure they saw us praying together on the plane."

"It sure seems costly to be a Christian here," K.J. said, pacing in front of the window.

Mindy took the camcorder now. "Is this the scariest outreach you've ever been on or what, Jeff?"

"I sure think so. But remember, this is what people in Communist countries go through all the time."

"What about Mr. Sanchez?" Mindy pleaded. "Can't we help him?"

Without hesitation, Jeff answered, "We have to."

"But how?" Mindy asked. "We'll just get in trouble, too."

"We can't just stay here and do nothing. Let's go down there."

"Wait," K.J. said. He was back at the window. "It's too late. They've handcuffed him and they're walking away with him."

Jeff saw that they needed a plan. Real fast.

"We'll follow them from a distance," he said calmly.

K.J. grabbed the camcorder and wrapped it in his jacket.

"Why are you bringing that?" Mindy asked.

"It may come in handy."

Once outside, they worked their way down the street, ducking in and out of doorways, always keeping the soldiers and Mr. Sanchez in sight. It was dark by the time they arrived in a deserted section of town.

The kids followed the soldiers into a fenced area of vacant lots and buildings that looked like they once had been factories. K.J. grabbed Jeff's arm and pointed. "Look, they're taking him into that old red brick building."

Jeff kept remembering that Warren had left him in charge of the team. Now he wrestled with the consequences of his actions. He was sure that helping Mr. Sanchez was the right decision. But how should they do it? He didn't want to risk the safety of the others.

He reached out his arm in front of K.J. and Mindy. "We've got to be careful. We don't want to make things worse. Maybe we should go back and get Warren."

"No," Mindy pleaded. "They might take him somewhere else. We'd never find them again."

Jeff couldn't argue with that.

It was really dark now. Jeff's hands were cold and clammy. As they crept up to the building, Jeff heard the twigs snapping under his feet.

"There's a light on in one of the rooms," Mindy said, pointing.

*If only we were home,* Jeff thought, *I'd just find a pay phone and call the police.* Nice plan in America. Not so easy here.

They made their way toward the lighted window, pressing themselves as close as they could to the side of the building. Then Jeff heard voices coming from the room.

"We'd better get down and crawl the rest of the way," he whispered. "Crouch down and try to make it to those bushes over there by the window."

"Let's just make sure Mr. Sanchez is okay," Mindy said. "Then we'll go back and get Warren." They all nodded.

"I'm gonna get as close as I can," Jeff said, "and try to catch what they're saying."

Jeff felt chilled to the bone even though the night air was warm. But he wasn't about to give up. While the others remained in the bushes, he made his way to a spot right under the open window. He could hear Mr. Sanchez' voice. And he heard his own name mentioned. It was easy to hear, because they were all yelling, but he couldn't understand them, because they were talking so fast and it was in Spanish.

He slid to the ground and crawled back over to the others. He was sure that his face betrayed his fear.

"They're talking about us. I distinctly heard them say my name."

Jeff looked at Mindy. She was trembling.

Jeff heard a faint noise, and glanced toward the window. K.J. was kneeling by the window, pointing his camcorder into the room, and he was recording!

"What are you doing?" he whispered hoarsely.

"I can record what they're saying on this."

"What good will that do?" Mindy whispered.

"It might help," K.J. said. He held the camera steady.

Jeff crawled back over to the window. He understood some Spanish; he might be able to piece some of their conversation together.

"Try to be quiet, K.J.," he urged, pushing him away. "I think I heard the word for plane....Wait a minute. They're saying something about a package."

The voices grew louder. Whack! Whack! Whack! And then some groans.

He couldn't just sit there and do nothing. He risked a peek in the window.

"Oh, no!" he whispered. "They're beating Mr. Sanchez with a hose!"

"Let's get outta here!" Mindy said.

"We can't just leave him here," Jeff said.

"There's nothing we can do," Mindy insisted.

K.J. turned around. "I'll bet if I could film the beating, we could use the tape to help Mr. Sanchez."

"Don't do it, K.J," Mindy whispered. "They'll hear you."

Jeff made a decision. "Go ahead. But be quiet."

K.J. raised the camcorder back into position. The whacks and groans were louder now. He held the camera steady and kept it running.

Mindy had joined the other two at the window. She pulled at K.J.'s arm. "That's enough! Let's go!"

K.J. turned the camcorder off and slid to the ground. Jeff glanced once more through the window before they left. He wasn't prepared for what he saw. He was staring straight into the eyes of an angry soldier!

Jeff jerked upright. "Let's get outta here quick. He saw me."

They took off running toward the other old factories, hoping to make it out of the fenced-in area to the main road. Then they heard the sound of heavy-booted feet pounding the ground behind them.

*We'll never make it!* Jeff thought. They ran from building to building, keeping out of the open as much as possible. Then Jeff spotted a large wooden shed almost obscured by trees.

"Over here!" he gasped as he led the way. "We can hide in this old shed. It's our only hope."

K.J. ran as fast as he could, clutching the camcorder in his jacket close to his chest. Mindy fell down twice trying to keep up, and Jeff stopped long enough to help her each time.

K.J. was the first one inside. Then Jeff. Finally, Mindy. Jeff pulled hard on the door and it shut firmly.

"We'll have to stay here now," he said. "I just hope they didn't see where we went."

"It's dark in here," Mindy said.

"Well, what did you expect, Mindy? It looks like this place hasn't been used for a long time."

They huddled together in the darkness. Jeff broke away from them and ran his hand along the wall. He almost tripped over some chairs, and he bumped his shin on an old desk. Then he discovered a large pile of wood stacked in the back of the shed.

"Come over here," he hissed. "We can hide behind this."

They crawled toward his voice. Now they could hear stomping and yelling outside. Through the small windows, they saw flashlight beams circling, penetrating the darkness. Jeff felt Mindy's hand on his arm. He was shaking almost as much as she was.

# Chapter 9

# Danger in the Darkness

Jeff pushed Mindy and K.J. flat against the floor. They pulled their knees up under their chins and curled into tight little balls.

The soldiers seemed confused. They kept walking around the shed, shouting to one another and waving their flashlights.

Jeff had never prayed so hard in his life. He decided he had to know what was going on outside, so he slithered along the floor until he reached a window. He slowly lifted himself up until he could see out. There was a soldier standing just a few feet away. But he was looking toward the other direction.

Jeff crawled back behind the wood pile just as the door flew open and two soldiers entered.

The soldiers' flashlights sliced through the darkness, and the kids tensed, sure that their hiding place had been revealed.

*Dear Lord,* Jeff prayed, holding his breath, *please don't let them find us. Please give us Your protection.*

The soldiers stood in the middle of the shed, backs together. Slowly they turned, searching every corner. Jeff watched as the flashlights shone on the old desk and chairs, creeping ever closer to the pile of wood. Finally, the wood was bathed in light. Jeff knew it was over. He almost stood up and raised his hands. Why weren't the soldiers yelling at them?

Then it was dark again.

The door closed.

They slowly exhaled in relief.

"I can't believe it. They must have been blind," K.J. said, giggling nervously. "They pointed their lights right at us!"

Jeff tiptoed over to one of the windows. "They're going away."

"Let's make a run for it," Mindy suggested.

"Not yet. There may be some more soldiers near the road. Let's wait a little longer."

"I want to go home," Mindy cried. "This isn't any fun. We could have been killed!"

"Did you catch anything they said in the building, Jeff?" K.J. asked.

"Yeah. I heard the words for kid and for camera. I think they're looking for a kid with a camera."

K.J. gulped.

"How long do we have to stay here?" Mindy asked.

"A little longer," K.J. jumped in quickly.

Mindy began to cry. "We should have waited for Warren. He would have known what to do."

"Sis, we had to try to help Mr. Sanchez. There wasn't time to wait for Warren."

Jeff moved to the door. He leaned on it slightly. This time it squeaked when it opened. He looked around and then closed it carefully.

"I still can't believe they missed us," K.J. said, shaking his head. "What happened, Jeff?"

Jeff had no time to explain. "K.J.," he said, "take the tape out of the camera."

K.J. ejected the tape and slipped it into his jeans pocket. He sure was glad their camcorders used such small tapes.

"We can't let them find us with that camera," Jeff said. "We've got to hide it somewhere."

Mindy looked at it in disgust. "I knew that thing would get us in trouble," she said.

"Far from it," Jeff assured her. "I don't think it will hurt us. And I know it will help Mr. Sanchez."

K.J. reluctantly agreed to leave the camcorder behind, and rewrapped it in his jacket. Jeff hid it in the bottom of the wood pile. Then he looked down at his watch, but it was too dark to see what time it was.

"The best thing to do is to wait a while longer," he said. "There's a fence all around this lot. They might have guards stationed where we came in."

"I'll bet Warren is wondering where we are," Mindy said.

"He probably thinks we're still at church," Jeff said.

"What about the package?" K.J. asked.

"You're right! He'll know we came back."

"He's probably out looking for us right now," Mindy said hopefully. "Maybe he'll call the police."

Both boys looked at her with raised eyebrows.

K.J. looked around. "I'm not that scared now," he said. He touched the videotape in his pocket. "Let's find a place to hide this thing, too."

Jeff thought about it a long time. "I don't think it's a good idea to hide the tape here."

"Why not?" K.J. asked.

"We might not be able to get back here. But if we split up, we can get the tape out for sure."

"I want to stay with you, Jeff," Mindy pleaded.

"No, Mindy. You go back to the hotel with K.J. I'll help you guys climb over the fence. You should be able to get back to the main road pretty easily."

"Where are you going?" Mindy asked.

"I'll go out the way we came in. I'll be a decoy. I can run faster than either of you. I'm sure I'll be able to outrun them even if they see me."

"Are you sure you trust me to take care of the tape?" K.J. asked.

"Yes, K.J., I trust you," Jeff said. "There's a lot riding on this. Take the tape back to Warren. If he isn't at the hotel, hide it."

This time K.J. opened the door. He peeked outside. Then he motioned for Jeff and Mindy to follow him. Jeff pointed the way to the wooden fence, and they walked as quietly as they could until they came to it. Jeff found a big box under a tree and dragged it over to the fence. One at a time, K.J. and Mindy scrambled up on the box and Jeff boosted them over the top.

"Will you guys be okay?" he asked, pressing his eye to a knothole. Mindy's eye was on the other side. She tried to convince him one more time, "Why don't you come with us?"

"I'll meet you back at the hotel as soon as I can. Now get outta here. Quick."

Jeff turned and hurried off in the other direction. He had only gone a few feet when he saw some soldiers coming right toward him. He had to think quickly. He could try to make it back to the fence. Or he could go way around them and try to get to the road. Or he could go back to the shack. He decided on the shack.

He pulled the door tightly behind him. He crouched back behind the lumber pile. The first thing he did was to check and make sure that the camcorder was still there.

Meanwhile, K.J. and Mindy inched their way along the fence.

"Do you think Jeff will be okay?" she asked K.J. anxiously. "I know he told us to go back to the hotel, but Jeff's my brother, and I love him. I don't want to leave him there alone."

"What do you want to do?" K.J. asked.

"I can't leave without him," Mindy cried. "Let's go back and look through that hole again. The moon is out now. Maybe we can see how far he's gotten."

K.J. hesitated. "Let's think about it first. I'm responsible for this tape now."

While they were discussing what to do, they heard loud shouts, then the sound of people running. A lot of people. Then they heard a voice that sounded like Jeff's.

They raced back to the knothole. Mindy got there first, and took off her glasses to put her eye close to the hole. She froze.

Jeff had been captured! His hands were already cuffed behind his back, and he was being shoved along a path by soldiers with rifles. One soldier was waving the camcorder in the air.

Mindy was gripped with terror. The soldiers were laughing at Jeff. Mean, cruel laughs. She distinctly heard one of the soldiers say, "Let's see how you like a night in a Cuban jail!"

# Chapter 10

# Captured

K.J. and Mindy stared at each other in disbelief.

They made their way along the fence as fast as they could. Soon they saw the main road, just as Jeff had said.

They hurried along the road, retracing their steps, darting from shadow to shadow. Mercifully, clouds had covered the moon and helped conceal their desperate flight. They were in a race against time. Jeff was going to jail! They had to get to Warren.

---

"Where is the tape?" one of the soldiers asked.

"I don't have it."

"Where is the blonde girl?"

"I don't know."

"Where are your other two friends?"

"I'm the only one here."

The soldier grabbed Jeff's arm in a vise-like grip. "Don't worry. Soon you'll tell us everything we need."

Jeff tried to stay on his feet, but he kept stumbling and being pushed to the ground. He risked a quick glance toward the fence. He hoped the others were a long way from there by now.

When they passed the familiar old red brick building, he looked for the room where Mr. Sanchez had been interrogated. The light was off now. Where was Mr. Sanchez?

Once they got to the main street, he was forced to sit cross-legged on the ground in the middle of the soldiers. When a curious crowd gathered, the soldiers shooed them all away. Within minutes, a gray-green van screeched up beside them. From the letters and numbers on its side, Jeff presumed it was some sort of military vehicle. The future was looking very bleak.

---

While K.J. and Mindy were rushing back to the hotel, they ran into a group of tourists they had seen in the lobby that morning. They recognized the young couple from Russia, and worked their way through the others over to them. Mindy struck up a conversation with the Russian lady.

"You look like you've been running," the woman said to Mindy.

"Yeah," Mindy said, attempting to cram some of her wayward hair back under the rubber band that had held it. "We decided to get some exercise."

"Where are your other friends?"

"Oh, one of them is back at the hotel. The other one is still running," she said, smiling wryly.

Mindy and K.J. walked right into the lobby in the middle of the group.

---

Jeff watched as four armed soldiers poured out of the sliding door of the van. They surrounded him and grabbed him roughly under his arms. Then they lifted him into the van.

Jeff's body crashed against the side of the van as it sped away. The faster they went, the more he bounced. Up and down, up and down on the long bench that ran the length of the van. The bumpy road indicated that they had left the downtown area.

A soldier sat on each side of him, and two others faced him from the bench on the other side. Their hands rested ominously on rifles lying across their laps. Their eyes never left his face.

When the van stopped, Jeff leaned forward and looked through the front window. They were at some sort of compound.

Jeff could see a number of low buildings surrounded by a high chain link fence. Rolls of barbed wire topped the fence. With a lump in his throat, he realized that it was a prison.

The driver rolled down his window and asked permission to enter. The large iron gates swung open.

———————

Once safely in the lobby, K.J. and Mindy quickly separated from the group.

They looked around for a place to hide the tape. For some strange reason, K.J. felt drawn to the huge portrait of Fidel Castro which dominated the lobby. He walked over to it and inspected it closely. He ran his hand along the side of the gold frame which surrounded it. On the right-hand side, near the bottom, he discovered a small opening where the portrait had separated from its wooden backing. While Mindy stood in front of him, he slipped the tape into the opening.

Then they hurried to the elevator and up to the sixth floor.

When the elevator stopped and the doors separated, they looked both ways, making sure the hall was empty before they got out.

They moved cautiously but quickly toward K.J.'s room, and knocked on the door softly, waiting for Warren to open it. No response. Nothing but silence came from the room.

"Do you think Warren might be in there and just not hear us?" Mindy asked hopefully.

"I don't know. We'll soon find out," K.J. answered and pulled a key from his pocket.

When they entered the room, it looked just the way they had left it.

"What if the soldiers came and arrested Warren?" Mindy asked anxiously.

K.J. refused to even discuss it. He and Mindy sat

down and stared at each other. They waited. They didn't know what to do next.

---

The door to the van was flung open and Jeff was pulled out. He was taken into an office within a large, old building. The soldiers removed his handcuffs, pushed Jeff into a chair, and left him to wait alone.

Jeff looked around the room. There was no way to escape. The window overlooking the prison yard was broken, but covered with iron bars. The floor was dirty, and the walls were yellow and cracked.

The door opened and a burly man in a rumpled uniform strode in. His hair was greasy and his eyes were half covered by puffy eyelids. A dark stubble covered the lower half of his face.

He pulled up a chair and scooted it close to Jeff. He lit a cigar, then blew smoke in Jeff's face. The officer glared at Jeff.

Finally, he leaned forward. "My name is Captain Roybal, and you're in real trouble."

"I've done nothing wrong, sir. Could I call a lawyer?"

Captain Roybal laughed.

"Then I want to contact my leader at the hotel."

Mr. Roybal ignored him.

"You are here because you have committed a crime against the Cuban government."

Jeff couldn't believe his ears. "I'm just a tourist."

"We have your video camera. What were you doing with a video camera?"

"We brought the camera to take pictures of your country for our high school. We want to learn more about your country."

"Why were you taking pictures of government business?"

"I don't remember seeing government business."

Captain Roybal sounded more impatient. "What do you know about a Mr. Sanchez?"

"Look, I'll be honest with you," Jeff said as he leaned forward. "I met Mr. Sanchez on the plane on our way here. He became my friend. When we saw him in front of the hotel, he seemed to be in some sort of trouble, so my friends and I followed him."

The captain jumped to his feet angrily. "And do you take a camera with you wherever you go?"

"We were told that camcorders are legal here."

"Why were you taking pictures of our discussion with Mr. Sanchez?"

"I told you. We thought he was in trouble."

"You must give us the video," the captain said.

"I don't know where it is," Jeff said honestly. He tilted his chair back.

"You can be tried for treason. If you are found guilty, you'll be locked up in prison for good. No one in America will be able to help you then."

The captain went on, "And what about your friends?"

Jeff slumped down in his chair, exhausted. Once more, he answered honestly, "I don't know where they are."

He sat up straight. He decided to tell Captain Roybal about the Reel Kids club.

Captain Roybal raised his eyebrows.

Jeff told him about their travels. He even told him about their work in churches.

Captain Roybal raised his eyebrows.

In desperation, Jeff said, "All right, then. Don't you have laws against putting 15-year-old boys in prison? That's not going to look good in the American press."

Captain Roybal became enraged. "We don't care about your American press. We have 15-year-old boys in our army.

"I'll let you go on one condition. Tell me where the video is," Captain Roybal said, standing over Jeff and staring down at him.

"I told you. I don't know where it is," Jeff said. "And that's the truth."

"Then you'll rot in a prison cell until you decide to cooperate."

---

Mindy took out her laptop computer and started pecking away on the keys while K.J. paced around the room. Then an idea seemed to hit them both at the same time. Mindy grabbed the phone even as K.J. reached for it. They would call home.

She had just dialed the operator when they heard a key turning in the lock. The door opened slowly. Warren walked in wide-eyed. "Where in the world have you guys been? I've been worried sick."

"We've been waiting for you," Mindy cried.

"I didn't get back from my meeting until almost seven. No one was here. I waited awhile and then went to the church to talk to Emmanuel. He said that you had left around 5:30. I've been looking for you everywhere."

Mindy couldn't take any more. Her chin quivered, and she burst into tears.

"What's wrong, Mindy?" Warren asked.

"You're not gonna believe this. Jeff's been captured by some soldiers!"

They filled Warren in on the events of the day, then he picked up the phone and asked for an outside line. They needed prayer support in a hurry. Almost an hour passed before a line became clear.

Of course, Jeff's parents wanted to fly right down to Havana, but Warren discouraged them from doing so. For one thing, it would be impossible for them to get visas that fast. Instead, he asked them to contact people to pray for Jeff.

As soon as Warren hung up the phone, Mindy flew into his arms and put her head on his shoulder, sobbing uncontrollably.

"Don't worry," Warren assured her. "God will tell us what to do."

"Meanwhile," Mindy wailed, "my brother is rotting in some prison!"

# Chapter 11

# The Cuban Prison

Jeff stared at Captain Roybal. He didn't like what he had just heard.

"I'm going to give you one last chance before you're locked up," the captain said. "Let's go over this once again. What's your purpose in coming here?"

"We're part of a Christian communications club at our high school. We get school credit for studying different countries."

Captain Roybal's voice became impatient. "Why do you try to force your religion on other people?"

Jeff's face lit up. "Captain Roybal, I believe everyone deserves a personal relationship with Jesus."

Captain Roybal put his face right in front of Jeff's. "Are you trying to convert me?"

Jeff didn't answer him directly. "The Lord has changed my life. He can change yours, too."

When Jeff started to tell him about the car accident, the captain grew fidgety. "Enough of this. Just tell me where the video is."

"I told you. I don't know."

"Then I have no other choice. You will be placed in a prison cell until you talk."

———

K.J. and Mindy went over everything again for Warren.

"Tell me once more exactly where the video is right now."

"It's right behind Fidel Castro. In the lobby."

"Then you haven't watched it yet?" Warren asked.

"No," K.J. answered.

"Then let's get our other camcorder and the monitor and go see what we've got," Warren said. "But we better watch it somewhere else. The police might show up here any minute."

———

Jeff stood in his undergarments. He was shaking, but not from cold. A guard handed him a gray jumpsuit. "Put your clothes in this bag," he ordered.

Jeff was fingerprinted and escorted down a long, tunnel-like corridor. Every door he passed had a tiny window with bars across it.

They stopped in front of one of the doors and the guard turned a key in the lock. Jeff had never seen a room so empty.

Torn newspapers covered the floor. A large metal shelf on one wall held a dirty blue and white mattress with the stuffing coming out of several holes. The cement block walls were cracked, and Jeff could see the night sky through a tiny window covered with bars at the top of the back wall. The cell had no toilet, only a big hole in the back corner of the floor.

The door clanged shut behind him.

Jeff sat down on the mattress. He heard cockroaches scurrying, and saw one disappear through a crack near the front of the cell. When he investigated, he heard the sounds of someone moving around.

Jeff put his ear near the crack and listened. The noise sounded more like a person than a cockroach.

Leaning closer, he called out, "Is anyone there?"

After a few seconds, he repeated the question.

"Is anyone there?"

He was astonished to be answered in English. "Who are you?"

"My name is Jeff Caldwell. I'm an American."

"My name is José Antonio Martinez Morales. Why are you in here?"

"I'm here because I filmed something."

"How's that?"

Jeff explained briefly. He was careful not to describe exactly what was on the video. Then he asked José to tell him something about the prison.

José told him the prison had been used since the Castro revolution to lock up political prisoners.

"How long have you been here?" Jeff asked.

"Since 1965. I was sent to prison because the authorities said I was a traitor to my country."

His story broke Jeff's heart. Here was someone who had experienced the revolution firsthand. In addition to losing his own freedom, his family had lost all their finances. He hadn't heard from any relatives in years.

Jeff began to understand why God had let him go to prison.

---

It was really late now, and it was pitch black behind the hotel. The team looked around to make sure they weren't being watched. They huddled together in an alcove near the kitchen entrance, and K.J. took the retrieved tape from his pocket. He placed it in the camcorder, then plugged in their little monitor. They all peered at the screen while K.J. pressed the playback button.

"Hey, this is better than I expected," K.J. said when the tape began to play.

There was Mr. Sanchez right there on the tape. Some soldiers were leaning over him and waving their fists at him. Then one of them slapped him. Another one picked up a piece of hose and began beating him. Mr. Sanchez put an arm up to ward off the blows. Mindy turned away.

They didn't dare risk hiding the tape in the lobby again. They looked for a new place, and K.J. spotted some uneven bricks in the back wall of the hotel. It would be a perfect place to stash it. Looking around once more to make sure they weren't being watched, K.J. quickly hid the tape.

They had barely gotten back to the room when a knock rattled the door. Mindy suggested hiding under the bed, but Warren went to see who it was. Two men in suits walked into the room.

"We want to see Mr. Russell."

"I'm Mr. Russell."

"We're with the police."

---

Jeff pulled the dusty mattress off its shelf and dragged it over near the crack in the wall. He sat down on it as José continued his story.

Jeff couldn't imagine what it would be like to spend more than 25 years in prison. It reminded him of the stories he'd heard about martyrs in the early Church who were imprisoned and persecuted.

"Do you think you'll ever get out of here?" Jeff asked.

"I had that hope burning in my heart for years. Now I've given up."

"How long do you think they'll keep me here?" Jeff asked.

"They're obviously trying to scare you. You must have something they want."

Jeff could tell how eager José was to talk to someone after all the years he had spent virtually alone. They talked most of the night. Jeff listened to everything José had to say, and then told his own story.

Warren invited the men into the room. The tall one got right to the point. "Your young friends have gotten themselves into plenty of trouble."

"I understand you have Jeff. I want to know where he has been taken," Warren said boldly.

"We're looking for a certain videotape that Mr. Caldwell had with him. I'm sure your friends here know what tape I'm referring to."

K.J. exhaled deeply. Mindy looked down at the floor and twirled her ponytail with her index finger.

"You have no right to keep Jeff in prison," Warren insisted.

"We have laws against what he did. He videotaped a top secret meeting."

"How do you know he did that?"

"We found the camera. But no tape. Your friends were with him. Why don't you ask them what happened to it?"

K.J. looked at Mindy. Mindy looked at K.J. Neither of them said a word.

"They don't have to answer your questions. I'm the one in charge."

"We'll give you till tomorrow morning to think."

"And what about Jeff?"

"He stays in jail."

# Chapter 12

# A Strange Twist

When the policemen left the room, Warren locked the door. "We need to spend time in prayer," he said. "God will give us a plan."

They huddled together in prayer. They prayed for Jeff and for Mr. Sanchez. K.J. even prayed for the soldiers. They would wait for God's direction. They would wait as long as it took.

Suddenly, Mindy opened her eyes. "I have an idea. If we can get that video to Los Angeles, we can make the Cuban government let Jeff go."

K.J. brightened. "Maybe Maria can help us. I got her phone number at the airport."

Warren said, "I don't think we can risk it."

K.J. shrugged his shoulders. "What else can we do? They're watching us like hawks."

"We can find a tourist going to Los Angeles. We can go out to the airport or something. Somebody has to take it to my parents," Mindy said.

"Yeah!" K.J. jumped up. "And your dad can play it on the news."

"I think you're on to something," Warren said.

Warren reached for his briefcase. He pulled out an airline schedule. "Let's see when the next flight leaves for L.A." He studied the schedule. "There's a flight tomorrow morning at six.

"Wait a minute! Remember that man from Los Angeles we met when we were checking in? Didn't he say he was going back home on the early flight Monday? Does anybody remember his name?"

They began wracking their brains. If only they could remember his name!

K.J. said, "I think it was something like a district. Or a county. Does that make sense?"

Mindy jumped up. "Ward! Ward! That was it. His name was Mr. Ward. Oh, Warren, do you think we could find him?"

Warren ran to the phone and dialed the hotel operator. When she came on, he asked to be connected to the room of Mr. Ward. It seemed hours before a very groggy man picked up the phone.

"Mr. Ward," Warren apologized. "I'm terribly sorry to bother you so late. I know you've got an early flight out in the morning. I'm Warren Russell. I met you Saturday night when we were checking into the hotel. I need to see you right away. It's urgent."

There was silence on the other end for a few seconds. Finally Mr. Ward asked, "What do you want me to do?"

"Could you possibly come to our room? It's number 626. I think it would be safer that way."

Shortly, there was a soft knock on their door.

Warren went over and put his head against the door. "Who's there?" he asked softly.

"Mr. Ward here."

Warren opened the door and glanced up and down the hall.

"What's the problem?" Mr. Ward asked as soon as he got in the room.

"I'm going to have to trust you with something very, very important. And I'm going to have to ask you to trust us. We have a videotape we have to get to Los Angeles. To Jeff's father at his TV station. Could you take it for us?" he pleaded.

Warren held the tape out to Mr. Ward. They waited for his answer.

"What's on the tape?" he asked.

Warren told him the truth. "Would you be willing to risk carrying it to L.A.? It may be the only way we can get our friend out of prison."

Mr. Ward hesitated only briefly before shoving the tape into his pocket. "I would be honored to. But first, I have to ask you a question. Why did you take a chance on me?"

"Easy," Warren said. "I saw your Bible."

---

Jeff fell asleep a little before daybreak. When he opened his eyes, a dim glow was just lighting his cell. He heard José moving about.

"Jeff," José said. "Are you awake? I want you to know something. If you hadn't come to jail, shared your story with me, and become my friend, I don't know what I would have done. I shall be forever grateful."

"José, have you thought much about God since you've been in here?"

"I used to. All the time when I was first locked up. But then as time went on, He seemed so far away. I haven't thought about Him in a long time."

Jeff's voice was strong. "I want to tell you something. God is not far away. He's there in that cell with you right now."

"How can I believe that, Jeff?"

"Just ask Him into your heart. You'll know."

A few minutes later, Jeff heard José begin to cry. He knew that his new friend was weeping for joy.

---

Jeff heard footsteps come down the corridor and stop in front of his door. He looked out to see two guards standing there.

One of them handed him a hard roll and a small cup of water. "You have ten minutes. Be ready."

When they came back, he followed them to the room where Captain Roybal was waiting.

"Enjoy your sleep last night?"

"Not much."

"Now do you want to tell us about the video?"

Jeff shook his head to clear his tired mind. "I told you, I don't know where it is."

"How long do you want to stay here?"

"Not long, sir. I've done nothing wrong."

"I just wanted to see if you've had a sudden recall of memory. And to tell you one more thing. We're going to arrest your friends, too, if we don't get that video today."

---

The knock on the wall came early Monday morning. Mindy could hear Warren saying, "Get up and come over here. We'll probably have visitors soon."

When she got there, Warren already had sweet rolls and juice on a room service tray on the table. The bright morning sun almost fooled her into thinking that everything was all right. That maybe it had all been a bad dream.

"I'll check to be sure Mr. Ward's plane took off on time," Warren said.

Warren kept getting a busy signal every time he tried the airline's number. While he was still holding the phone, there was a knock on the door.

"I'm going to stall for more time," Warren whispered as he hung up and headed for the door.

It was the same two men who had been there the night before. Warren smiled as he invited them in. "Please have a seat. I'll give you some information about the video."

"We don't want to sit down, and we don't want information. We want the video." The tall man was doing all the talking.

Warren ignored him. "I'm getting some information about it in a few hours. I can tell you then."

"Why can't you tell us now?"

"Someone else has it. I'm not sure where it is right now. But, I'll let you know as soon as we find out. We want Jeff back as soon as possible," Warren said.

"If you try to trick us, you won't see your friend again," the shorter one said as they left the room.

After locking the door behind them, Warren rushed back to the phone. He patiently dialed the number over and over until he finally got through.

"Did Cuban Air flight 221 leave on time?"

K.J. looked smug. Mindy crossed her fingers.

The answer came back. "I'm sorry. That flight has been delayed. It should depart in just a few minutes."

Warren glanced at his watch. It was almost eight o'clock. He needed to stall until Mr. Ward could clear customs in Merida.

---

They could hear footsteps approaching their room again. It was 11:00 a.m. Warren wanted to stall them for at least another half hour. He could only hope that Mr. Ward was all right.

"I'm sorry, but there has been another delay. We'll have to wait just a little longer before I can give you the information you want," Warren said when the men came in.

"What is the delay this time?" the tall man demanded.

"I promise to let you know where the tape is soon."

They all sat down and waited. After a while, one of the men got up and paced the room. When he sat down, K.J. took up the pacing.

Warren kept checking his watch. When it was a little past 11:30, he said, "I can tell you now."

Both men stood up. "Where is it?"

"A friend took it with him on the first flight out of here this morning. It'll play on TV stations all over America if Jeff isn't released at once."

Mindy grinned smugly. She couldn't wait for their reaction. She knew they'd explode.

They looked at each other. They didn't say a word for a few minutes. When one of them did speak, it wasn't at all what Mindy had expected.

The short one reached into his briefcase and pulled a videotape out. He shook it in Warren's face and then threw it on the table.

"Sorry. Your little trick didn't work. We took the tape away from your friend at the airport!"

# Chapter 13

# Free for Now

When Jeff was returned to his cell, he couldn't wait to continue his conversation with José.

He leaned against the wall near the crack and knocked on the wall. "José, I'm back."

There was no response. He called again. "José?" Still no response. He decided that José had fallen asleep, and decided to try again a little later.

When almost an hour had gone by, he tried again. And again. Silence. In despair, he realized that the cell next door was empty.

He sat on his tattered mattress filled with remorse. The team's outreach mission was in jeopardy because of his arrest. Mr. Sanchez had been arrested and beaten because of his witness. And now José was probably in trouble because of his association with Jeff. It wasn't supposed to work out this way.

He felt completely helpless. He had never needed to depend on God's grace more. Maybe that was what this was all about.

---

The color drained from Warren's face. He picked up the tape and looked it over. "How do we know that this is our tape?"

The policeman laughed. "It looks like your tape, doesn't it?"

Warren looked at K.J. and K.J. shrugged. "That's the kind we use."

"Let's play it to be sure," Mindy suggested.

"The tape contained top secret information. We've already erased it."

Mindy looked the tall man right in the eye. "That tape was not government business. It was evidence. It showed your people beating Mr. Sanchez!"

Mindy had let it slip out right in front of the policemen! She gasped in horror.

The policeman smiled. "We're going to carry on an investigation for the next few days. You Americans like justice? You'll get your justice. On Thursday, you'll be taken to court and tried for conspiracy against our country."

"Does that mean we're going to jail now?" K.J. asked in a subdued tone.

"Not now. You're free until Thursday."

"What about Jeff?" Warren asked.

"He will be released this afternoon. He'll be tried on separate charges Thursday morning. Your trial is Thursday afternoon. Until then, you can do as you want.

"One more thing, you are not to talk about this to anyone. And one of our agents will be with you at all times."

"I want to call a lawyer in Los Angeles," Warren said.

"No more unauthorized calls."

Warren began to digest the news. He said, "We've got meetings scheduled in churches. Can we still go?"

"You may continue your schedule. But you've already missed your group's trip to the beach this morning. Another thing, you must write down everything you plan to say at these churches and give it to our agent. It must be approved in advance."

"When can we see Jeff?" Mindy asked.

"You can go with our agent to pick him up at the prison this afternoon. While you're there, take a good look around."

The policeman walked over and opened the door, motioning for someone to come in.

"Meet Pedro Ramirez. He'll go everywhere you go from now on."

Mr. Ramirez was about the same age as Warren. He was not much taller than K.J., and looked like he'd enjoyed some good meals. He was dressed casually in a short-sleeved blue cotton shirt and dark blue cotton slacks. His weight, combined with the Havana heat, had already caused dark, wet patches of sweat to appear on his shirt.

"Mr. Ramirez," Mindy demanded, "when can we get my brother?"

He gave Mindy a cold stare. "We'll get him when I'm ready. I'm in charge now."

Mr. Ramirez led them to the parking lot and pointed to an official-looking van. Within minutes, they were headed out of the city down a bumpy road.

Warren sat in the front seat and asked their driver, "How long have you been a Communist?"

"I have been with the party 15 years now."

Mindy leaned over the seat. "Do we have to call you Mr. Ramirez?"

He softened a little. "We'll be spending a lot of time together; you can call me Pedro."

"You're nicer than the others. Why is that?" Mindy asked.

Pedro half smiled. "I was told to let you go about your business. As long as you do as you're told, we'll get along fine."

"Do you think your court will find us guilty?" Mindy asked.

"You broke our laws. You have to pay the price."

"Like going to prison?" she pressed.

"I'm not your judge. I'm just an agent in charge of watching you."

Pedro veered off the highway and headed for a compound surrounded by a high fence. Barbed wire circles ran along the top of the fence. He stopped at a guardhouse and thrust an identification card out the window. The guard examined it and went back inside his shelter. A few minutes later, the large iron gates swung open.

As they drove through the compound, Mindy whispered to K.J., "This place gives me the creeps."

"It's too bad I didn't bring my camera," K.J. whispered back.

She gave him a dirty look.

They followed Pedro into one of the oldest-looking buildings on the grounds, down a long hall, and into a private office. They didn't have long to wait before a man in a wrinkled uniform came in. He looked like he could use some sleep, not to mention a shave. But he was obviously the boss.

"I'm Captain Roybal. Jeff will be out soon."

"Is he okay?" Mindy asked.

"We have taken good care of him. I understand I might be seeing the rest of you later this week."

Just then, Jeff came through the door.

Mindy jumped out of her chair and threw her arms around him. "I wasn't sure I would ever see you again."

Jeff breathed a sigh of relief. He smiled at his three teammates. "You guys are a welcome sight."

Mindy asked Jeff, "How are you doing?"

"I could use a little food and sleep, but I'm okay."

Pedro spoke to Captain Roybal in Spanish for a few minutes before the captain said they could go.

"Is it all right if I leave a note for my friend José?" Jeff asked bravely.

"As long as it isn't anything religious."

Jeff asked Mindy for a pen and paper and quickly wrote out a note of encouragement. He knew it would be checked, so he worded it carefully and reread it before he folded it and handed it to Captain Roybal.

"Can I ask you something?" he asked the captain. "What happened to José? He's not in his cell."

Captain Roybal hesitated, then seemed to make a decision. "We brought him in for questioning. We thought you might have told him something about the tape. He's back in his cell now."

When they were in the van, Jeff asked Pedro, "Am I allowed to discuss my time in jail?"

"Say whatever you want to each other. But remember that I'll be listening."

Jeff told the others what had happened to him.

Mindy's eyes got wide. "Did you see any rats in there?"

"No, but lots of cockroaches. That place is old."

He started to tell them about José, but caught himself before he said too much. He decided it would be better to wait until they were alone.

Then K.J. told Jeff about the video. Jeff sank down in his seat and looked out the window, trying not to show how upset he was. He had counted on that tape to buy their freedom.

# Chapter 14

# On the Beach

When they got back to the hotel, Jeff said, "I never thought anything could look so good."

Pedro pulled in the back parking lot, and K.J. quietly pointed out to Jeff the spot in the wall where they had stashed the tape. As soon as they were out of the van, Mindy asked, "Can we eat now? I'm hungry. And I'm sure Jeff is, too."

"Is that so?" Pedro said as he glanced at his watch. "It's only 4:30."

"We'll take you with us, Pedro," K.J. offered.

"You have no choice," Pedro answered, breaking into a wide grin for the first time. "I'll be with you

113

every minute until Thursday."

"Even at night?" Mindy asked.

"At night, you'll be locked in your rooms. Someone will be stationed just outside your doors. I'll sleep across the hall."

"Oh, that's great," K.J. said sarcastically. "Hey, you better be careful spending so much time with us. Next thing you know, you'll be joining our club."

Warren said, "I could use a little rest before dinner. What say we go eat about seven o'clock?"

Pedro looked at his watch and agreed. "I'll come upstairs and lock you in."

When Jeff heard the sound of the key turning, he realized he was still a prisoner. He was eager to talk to Warren. "What happened to Mr. Ward?"

"I don't know. He's probably being held somewhere. Maybe we can find out from Pedro."

The team insisted that Jeff tell them in great detail what had happened to him in the prison. He especially enjoyed telling them about José and how they should all be praying for him. Then they talked about Mr. Sanchez.

Suddenly, Mindy jumped up. "We're not thinking straight. Let's just call Mom and Dad."

She picked up the phone and dialed the operator. She looked puzzled, hung up, and tried again. Then she handed the phone to Warren. "There's something the matter with this thing."

"They've disconnected it," Warren said. "There's no way we can get word out now."

"Can't we use another phone?" Mindy asked.

"How? Did you forget about Pedro?"

"Well, at least if we don't show up at the airport Friday, your parents will know something's wrong," Warren said.

"What do you all think of Pedro?" Jeff asked.

Mindy grinned. "I like him. He's kinda cute and he's nice. I think I'm getting to his heart," she kidded.

"I hope you're right. But remember, be careful what you say."

---

It was 7:00 when Pedro knocked on the door. Jeff was more than ready for a decent meal. Prison food left a lot to be desired.

"Do you know any good restaurants in Havana?" Warren asked Pedro.

Pedro looked insulted. "I know a restaurant that serves good Cuban food. It's close to here," he said.

Pedro led them down the street. They frequently had to step aside to avoid being hit by rambunctious children playing on the sidewalks. Many people were out enjoying an evening stroll.

Jeff didn't know if his imagination was working overtime or not, but he sensed a lot of people staring at him. He mentioned it to Pedro, who shrugged. "Just ignore it. Remember, you're not allowed to discuss anything with anybody."

When they were in the restaurant, even the wait-ress looked at Jeff strangely as she led them to a booth and passed out menus.

*She knows something,* Jeff thought.

When the waitress came back to take orders, she asked Jeff, "Aren't you the American everybody is talking about?"

"Excuse me! We would like to order now!" Pedro snapped angrily. He was blotting his forehead with one of the paper napkins and fanning himself with his menu. "We came here to eat, not talk."

Jeff wondered what the waitress knew. And how many other people knew something about him? What was God's purpose for his sudden notoriety? He tried to keep reminding himself that God was still in charge and had everything under control.

The waitress returned with sizzling char-broiled steaks for Jeff and Pedro and baked chicken for the others. She set big bowls of steaming rice, refried beans, and a green salad in the middle of the table.

When Jeff cut into his steak, a brownish red gravy flowed out. One bite and he rolled his eyes. He loved the spicy tomato and onion flavor. He couldn't remember when anything had tasted so good.

They ate in silence for awhile before Jeff turned to Pedro. "What do you think of us, Pedro?"

"Too fanatical. It'll get you in trouble."

Jeff cut into his steak again. He waited for one of the others to respond.

"We're not embarrassed about what we believe," Mindy said. "I've studied some about Communists. They're pretty radical themselves."

Pedro countered, "Everyone thinks his way is the best. Communism is the answer to man's selfishness."

The waitress began clearing some of the dishes,

and Mindy changed the subject. "Let me tell you about our club."

Jeff beamed as he listened to Mindy talk about the club. Then she talked about what the Bible meant to her. She even attempted to explain God's plan of redemption to Pedro.

"Man broke his relationship with God because of sin. That was the beginning of the selfishness you were talking about," Mindy said.

"So how is Jesus different from Marx? Or even Castro?"

"Jesus is different because He still lives even though He died. He's different because He's God's only Son. And God is going to get us out of this mess we're in."

Jeff couldn't believe his ears. Mindy was easily fielding Pedro's toughest questions. Where were these bold answers coming from?

When they were ready to go, Jeff cleared his throat. "You were right about the food, Pedro," he said pleasantly.

"Well, you better hope you are right about your God."

All the way back to the hotel, Mindy kept talking to Pedro about God. Jeff could tell she was determined to crack through the tough shell Pedro had built around himself. For once, Jeff was proud of her stubborn nature.

When Pedro started to lock Mindy in her room, she began to panic. "Do you have to lock me in, Pedro? What if there's a fire?"

"Don't worry. Remember, I'll be sleeping right across the hall. And another man will be sitting out here watching your rooms. Nothing can get in to harm you. And no one can get out."

———————

Jeff punched the snooze button on his alarm, even though he knew he should get up. Bright sunshine was pouring in the window and right onto his face.

"What's on our schedule for Tuesday?" he asked Warren sleepily.

"The beach."

"Hey, that sounds great," K.J. said, jumping out of bed. "We missed the beach trip yesterday."

"Why don't we go on a prayer walk at the beach?" Jeff suggested.

"You guys go. I just want to catch a few rays," K.J. said.

"I'll tell you what, Jeff," Warren said, "You and I can do that and let K.J. and Mindy just relax with Pedro if they want to."

Jeff remembered some of the prayer walks he'd gone on before. Wherever they walked, they claimed the land for the Lord. He wanted to claim part of the beach for the Lord.

The team put jeans and shirts on over their swimsuits, then grabbed their gear and headed down to the lobby. In the elevator, they tried to prepare themselves for the onslaught of questions they expected from Mr. Franko and the other group members. They needed to come up with an explanation for their absence the day before.

Fortunately, the other tourists stood apart from them and eyed them suspiciously while waiting for the bus to arrive. By now, more than one of them had to be convinced that these kids were up to something.

The bus pulled up, and Mr. Franko stepped out, his shirt ablaze with pink flamingos. He ushered the group onto the bus, not asking a single question. Jeff guessed that he had been instructed not to be too nosy.

As the bus bounced along, Mindy slid across the seat to be closer to Jeff. "I'm proud of you, Jeff."

"I'm proud of you, too. I wish I could have taped you last night."

"No more taping, please," Mindy kidded. "What's gonna happen to us, Jeff?"

"I don't want to scare you, but we need to prepare for the worst."

---

K.J. had his head stuck out the window before the bus even pulled off the road and onto the beach. Jeff saw that the surf was high, with waves crashing against the sand. *Just the way I pictured it*, he thought.

The bus emptied fast. K.J. raced Mindy to a spot on the beach where they quickly stripped to their swimsuits, ready to head for the water. Pedro huffed and puffed along behind them.

Mr. Franko assembled everyone at an old life-guard stand. "We'll meet at the bus at 12:45. We're scheduled to be back at the hotel by one o'clock, and you'll have the afternoon free."

Jeff asked Pedro, "Do you mind if Warren and I go for a short walk?"

"Don't get out of my sight."

Warren and Jeff stayed close to the edge of the water and let it splash over their bare feet. They stopped to look at an unusual shell once in awhile, but mostly they just talked, prayed, and sang hymns softly, praising God as they walked along.

"Lord," Jeff said, "I pray for all those who visit this beach. May the beauty that they see here cause them to see You better."

"Lord," Warren prayed, "Take control of this nation. You brought freedom to Russia. Bring it here."

Jeff turned to Warren. "I can't forget about Mr. Sanchez. I wonder where he is now. He was just beginning a new life, and he was full of hope for his country. He talked about a new revolution taking place here."

"Let's pray that it comes true."

Jeff looked back up the beach. He could see that K.J. was getting out of the water and drying himself off. Mindy was still sitting next to Pedro, gesturing in earnest conversation. They had walked so far that they'd have to hurry to make it back in time. They began running, and as they ran, something made Jeff glance over his shoulder at a group of tall palms clustered together. Standing in the shade was a familiar figure.

Mr. Garcia was back.

# Chapter 15

# The Crowd

Patches of fine sand trailed behind the team across the lobby, up the elevator, and into their rooms.

Jeff lingered in the shower too long; now he'd have to hurry. Pedro had agreed to take them shopping at Mindy's pleading.

When Jeff came out of the bathroom, he quickly pulled on jeans, a T-shirt, and tennis shoes. The other guys were already dressed.

Pedro and Mindy were waiting in the hall. "Is everyone ready? I'll show you a good place to buy ice cream when we get to the market."

"That's nice," Mindy said. "I love ice cream."

"Well, Cuba is famous for it," Pedro said proudly.

The guys sat together in the back of the van. Mindy was up front with Pedro.

When they got to the marketplace, they headed straight for the ice cream shop. Mindy was having a hard time choosing from the colored pictures of sundaes and cones on the menu. She kept turning back to the banana split.

"Everything looks too good," she said. When they had their orders, Pedro led them to a table.

While Mindy scooped her ice cream out of the dish, she asked for the umpteenth time, "Pedro, what are they are going to do with us?"

"I'm sorry, I'm not supposed to talk about it."

"They can't put Americans in prison, can they?"

"I'm afraid they can. But if you tell the truth at your hearing on Thursday, they may go easy on you."

"Will you help us?" Mindy pleaded.

"I have no influence in our court system. But I wish you the best."

Jeff suggested, "We'd better start shopping. We don't have much time before we have to get ready for the church service tonight."

"We'll take the van tonight instead of walking," Pedro offered. "It'll save us some time."

"Oh, yeah! You're going to church with us, aren't you?" Mindy said.

"He goes everywhere with us!" K.J. reminded her.

———

As they were driving to the service that night, Jeff said, "Pedro, I have to call my parents. Could we find a pay phone?"

"I'm sorry. You know I have strict orders."

"But my parents don't even know what's going on," Jeff pleaded.

"Just let us make one phone call," Mindy said. She was sitting next to Pedro again.

"I'm sorry. It's not up to me."

When they got close to the church, Jeff's mouth fell open. He couldn't believe how many young people were waiting on the sidewalk out front. They spilled over into the street. Were they at the right place? he wondered.

It was a completely different scene from Sunday's meeting. There was no way all those people would get into that small building.

"Where did all these people come from?" Jeff asked.

"A lot of people have heard about you," Pedro said. "Word travels fast in Havana. Especially when it has to do with Americans."

"Is that why they're here?" Jeff asked.

"Who knows? Some of them are probably just curious. We'll have extra agents here tonight."

"Will they still let us speak?"

"As long as you write out what you're going to say. And, please, don't change anything." Mindy and K.J. gave Pedro their speeches.

"We did ours this afternoon," she said, and they got out to mingle with the crowd while Jeff and Warren stayed in the van to finish working on theirs. Jeff was in charge of the service and would speak first. He handed his and Warren's text to Pedro on their way into the church, and went to find the pastor.

"There must be over 300 kids here," Jeff said.

"How many people do you normally have?" Warren asked the pastor.

"About 50. I've never seen anything like this."

The pastor asked everyone to be seated, and opened the service with a short prayer. Then another man stood and led the singing. Meanwhile, it was standing room only, and people were still coming in. They packed together as tightly as they could. Additional wooden benches were carried in.

Jeff could see that God had big plans for the evening. As the crowd grew, Jeff realized that most of them wouldn't be there if he hadn't become famous by being arrested. God had known what He was doing all along.

When Jeff was introduced, he scanned the room. He could see uniformed soldiers scattered through the crowd. The rest of the team was sitting in the front row along with Pedro.

"It's good to be here..." Jeff spoke slowly. Emmanuel interpreted for the crowd. Jeff saw Mr. Garcia standing in the back, but he wasn't about to let anything distract him from God's purpose tonight. Once more, he shared about his brush with death and how he had asked Jesus into his life.

He avoided looking at Mr. Garcia. Instead, he concentrated on thinking about the hungry hearts of his audience. He could tell they longed for a message.

After Jeff had finished, he invited his sister to come up. He could tell that Mindy was eager to share her story, especially since Pedro was in the audience.

"I love Jesus more than anything in the whole world," she began, and some of the people applauded. She smiled her broadest smile, and her teeth gleamed and her braces flashed. Jeff turned to watch Mr. Garcia's reaction. He stood still, staring only at Mindy. There was real hatred on his face.

"I wish that everyone could know that same love," she continued. She was looking directly at Pedro now. Pedro's face had a big smile on it.

When it was K.J.'s turn, he began by telling the Cuban people how much he loved them. *This wasn't what he had written down,* Jeff thought apprehensively. He hoped it wouldn't cause any trouble. The message K.J. delivered came straight from his heart.

Before K.J. sat down, he invited Warren to come up. K.J. said, "Once in a while you meet someone who touches your life deeply. Two people have done that for me: Jesus and Warren Russell."

Jeff couldn't help wondering if this was the same guy who nearly didn't get to come on the trip because of a silly prank. He was really changing!

"This man started our club and named it the Reel Kids. He not only helped us develop our communication skills, but he helped us become 'real kids.'"

When Warren came up, he repeated the story of the club's origin and purpose. He challenged the young people in the audience. Jeff became alarmed, and looked over at Pedro. Warren was going way beyond his notes.

Pedro seemed more interested in listening to Warren than in making sure he stuck strictly to his approved text. Jeff noticed that Mr. Garcia had pulled the pastor aside and was arguing with him.

The pastor came to the platform, tapped Warren on the shoulder, and whispered something in his ear. Warren stepped aside. Mr. Garcia was leaning against the back wall, watching them closely.

Jeff was astounded by the pastor's bold words, spoken in Spanish, then interpreted into English for them by Emmanuel. He began, "My heart has been deeply moved tonight." He wiped his eyes.

"Our country is in deep trouble. This group has come to bring us an important message. The good news is that Jesus is the answer to our country's problems." The pastor's words rang with authority.

What would Mr. Garcia do now? Jeff knew he must be furious. When the pastor invited everyone to come forward and pray for the team, Mr. Garcia stormed out the door.

Pedro sat riveted to his chair, watching everything going on. He didn't join the crowd, but he did nothing to stop them.

Then the pastor invited everyone into the next room for cake and cookies. While they ate, the Reel Kids were bombarded with questions. Emmanuel stuck close to them, helping translate for those who didn't speak English.

Then Jeff noticed that Pedro had disappeared.

When he looked out the window, he could see trouble brewing.

Pedro and Mr. Garcia were standing in the middle of the street yelling at each other. Mr. Garcia had his fists up. Jeff turned and began moving through the crowd, looking for Warren.

## Chapter 16

# Sugar Cane Fields

**A** few minutes later, a hand grabbed Jeff's shoulder and spun him around.

Pedro was standing there with a frightened look on his face. "Mr. Garcia wants to see the team right away. He didn't like what Warren or the pastor said."

Clutching his Bible for security, Jeff gathered the team in a small side room. Mr. Garcia stormed in the room and slammed the door.

"We gave you permission to speak only if you agreed to follow our guidelines."

"What did we do wrong?" Warren asked innocently.

"You didn't stick to what you were supposed to say," Mr. Garcia said, waving the notes. "You tried to stir up the crowd."

"I'm sorry," Warren said. "I figured we were going to jail anyway, so it wouldn't make much of a difference."

"This charge will be added to the others against you," Mr. Garcia said. "You're getting yourselves in deeper and deeper."

They drove back to the hotel in silence. Pedro didn't look at any of them, and Mindy kept her eyes on the floor.

———————

When Jeff woke up the next morning, the first thing he saw was Warren packing his bag.

He shot up in bed. "Warren, are you going home or something?"

"No. Just getting organized."

Jeff smiled. "It was pretty quiet on the way home last night, wasn't it?"

"I hope Pedro will be all right. I didn't mean to get him in trouble," Warren said as he jotted some things down in his notebook.

"We'll find out this morning, won't we?" Jeff said.

"I'm praying that God will touch Pedro's heart. Did you notice how closely he was listening last night?" Warren asked.

"That was worth all we've been through. And can you believe how many people showed up?"

Jeff hurried to dress so he could have some time for prayer. There was still a little time before the tour.

When Pedro came in, he said right away, "You got me in trouble. Tonight, stick to the notes."

Pedro was quiet for a moment. "I've been thinking about what you said last night."

Mindy leaned forward. "And?"

"You guys really believe that stuff, don't you?"

"With all our hearts," Jeff said.

"I would like to take you to meet my parents today. My father has always been a sugar cane farmer. He's very ill. Would..." Pedro had a hard time getting the words out. "Would you pray for him?"

Jeff raised his eyebrows. "We'd be happy to."

"I'll take you this afternoon after your tour."

As they walked through old Havana on the tour, Jeff thought about all the people who had walked those same streets. Communism had ruled for more than 30 years, but not much progress had been made.

Jeff noticed that Pedro and Mindy were often in deep conversation as they walked together. Pedro seemed to be asking a lot of questions. Jeff was thrilled. It looked like Mindy was about to lead someone to the Lord for the first time.

When the tour bus dropped them back off at the hotel, Pedro looked at his watch. "Let's rest for a while. We'll go to my parents' house around 2:00."

In the elevator, Jeff asked Pedro, "Do you think we made our situation worse last night?"

"Not really. They already had a strong case against you."

"Pedro, can you tell us what happened to our friend at the airport?" Jeff asked.

"I'm not allowed to talk about it."

"Can we ask you just one other question? Why are they trying us separately tomorrow?"

"You are charged with different crimes. Jeff is in the most trouble. The rest of you will just be tried as his accomplices."

Pedro locked them in their rooms. When he returned at 2:00, Mindy said, "I can't wait to meet your family."

Once out of the city, they saw nothing but miles of sugar cane fields and farmhouses. Pedro told them that sugar cane was the backbone of the Cuban economy. He stopped the van in front of a small house. "This is where my parents live."

"How long have they lived here?" Mindy asked.

"As long as I can remember. All the farms are run by the government."

"I read about that. Does the system work?"

"It was okay until the Soviet Union pulled out and stopped buying our sugar. It destroyed our economy."

The team followed Pedro up to the porch where a small woman stood waiting. It was impossible to guess her age. Her skin had obviously been prematurely thickened and wrinkled by constant exposure to the sun.

"This is my mother," Pedro said proudly, putting an arm around her shoulders. She beckoned them in and offered them cold drinks.

Pedro talked with his mother in Spanish as he gestured toward the back of the house. Then he turned to the team to explain.

"My mother says that my father isn't doing too well. He has a high fever. I told her that you said your God has power to heal, and that you will pray for him." Pedro smiled. "She was surprised that I talked about religion with you."

"We may have some more surprises for her!" Mindy told the others quietly.

Pedro led the team to a back room where a frail, elderly man was stretched out on a small bed. He was covered with a thin sheet.

Pedro exchanged a few words with his father, then told the team, "When I told him you came to pray for him, he wanted to know when I started believing in prayer. I told him I'd changed a lot since getting to know the four of you." He smiled again.

Jeff gently placed his hand on the head of Pedro's father as the others gathered around the bed.

Jeff prayed simply, "Lord, I pray for Your healing hand to touch Pedro's father. Take this sickness from him, and let this family know how much You love them."

Mindy moved over to the bed and leaned down to hug Pedro's father. Jeff knew that her conversations with Pedro were the reason they were there.

Pedro's father opened his eyes and tried to form a smile for Mindy. Tears rolled down Pedro's cheeks. He squeezed Jeff's hand and thanked them all. Then they turned and tiptoed out of the room.

In the kitchen, Pedro said, "I want to tell you something. I felt something stirring in me when you prayed. I felt surrounded by love. Real love."

"It was the love of God that you felt," Warren said. He tapped on the kitchen table. "It's as real as this table.

"I didn't want the feeling to go away," said Pedro.

"It never has to," said Warren.

---

On the way back to town, Jeff felt brave enough to say something to Pedro. "Now do you understand why we came here?"

"I think I'm just beginning to understand. I wish there was something I could do to help you."

"You could pray for us," Mindy said.

---

The team's last speaking engagement was scheduled for Wednesday night, and once again, Jeff felt that the Lord had assembled the large crowd. "We won't get you in trouble tonight," he promised Pedro.

"I trust you. But it doesn't matter so much to me anymore."

The team followed God's leading, and He opened up more hearts to hear their message. The Reel Kids never tired of telling their stories; each event seemed to come alive with each retelling. Jeff knew that the stories of God's working in their lives would always be powerful. Powerful enough to start a revolution.

# Chapter 17

# Confession Time

It was Thursday, but Jeff wasn't sure he was ready for Thursday.

He knew he would need extra strength to get through the day. When he opened his Bible to Luke, his spirit rose. He read, "You will be brought before kings and governors, and all on account of my name....But make up your mind not to worry beforehand how you will defend yourselves. For I will give you words and wisdom that none of your adversaries will be able to resist or contradict...."

"Warren, K.J., listen to this." Jeff read the words to them. "I know God will be in that courtroom."

The team gathered for prayer before Pedro came to get them at nine o'clock. Jeff's trial was scheduled for 9:30.

"I still don't see why we can't all be tried at the same time," K.J. said.

"They're up to something. That has to be why we're being tried separately," Warren said.

When they heard a knock, Mindy threw open the door, anxious to talk to Pedro some more. Pedro was standing there, all right. Right behind Mr. Garcia.

"I'm here for Jeff," Mr. Garcia said, his bushy mustache twitching.

Jeff felt a cold sweat break out on his forehead.

"Can we go with you?" Mindy asked in a barely audible voice as Mr. Garcia grabbed Jeff's arm and led him from the room.

"You're going later."

"Please?" Mindy begged.

"It's okay, Mindy. I'll be fine," Jeff reassured her.

"You'd better say goodbye to him. You may not see him for a long time," Mr. Garcia said, laughing grimly. He pulled Jeff through the door.

As he walked out, Mr. Garcia turned to Pedro. "Keep an eye on them. Or you might find yourself in a cell next to them."

Mindy asked Pedro, "Why didn't they let us go?"

"They don't give me reasons."

"When will we see him again?"

"Jeff is on his way to a Cuban courtroom. He'll get a fair hearing based on our laws."

"What does that mean?" asked Warren.

"It means our government makes its own rules."

---

The van stopped at a building that looked much like any courthouse in the United States. Jeff followed Mr. Garcia inside, praying every step of the way.

They entered a small room where he was told to be seated.

"How confident do you feel now?" Mr. Garcia asked. "We got rid of lots of people like you during our revolution."

"What kind of people are you talking about?"

"People who need some kind of religious crutch."

Jeff sat quietly and wrestled with his thoughts. He made a decision: He would take full responsibility for everything that had happened. That was the only way the others might be spared.

---

When Mindy checked her watch, she realized it was already 12:30.

"Is Jeff's hearing over yet?" she asked Pedro. "It should be over by now."

"It usually doesn't take very long," he said.

"Why's that?" K.J. asked.

"The judges usually have their minds made up ahead of time. Under our system of law since the revolution, you are considered guilty until proven innocent."

"Then what's the use of having a trial?" Mindy asked.

"It's a formality," Pedro said. "We need to get going now. Your hearing starts in 30 minutes."

When they got close to the courthouse, Mindy turned to Pedro. "I can't bear the thought of never seeing my parents again." She began to cry.

Pedro didn't answer her, but she noticed that he had crossed his fingers. Just then, Warren spotted an old building next to the courthouse.

"What's that building?" he asked Pedro idly.

"That's the oldest hotel in the city."

"You mean it's still in use?"

"Some tourists still love to go there."

Warren stopped short. "Can I ask you for one last favor? Would you mind if I went over there and looked at it? I'll be right back."

Pedro looked at his watch. "I'll give you five minutes."

Warren took off running toward the hotel.

Pedro looked at his watch nervously. "I hope he comes right back. It'll be much worse for the rest of you if he doesn't."

Warren returned just as two soldiers came out of the courthouse to get them. They were taken into one room and Pedro into another.

Mindy nervously twirled her hair. K.J. ran a comb through his. "I wonder where Jeff is?" he asked.

"We'll find out soon," Warren said.

Pedro came into the room and scooted a chair up right next to Mindy's. He leaned over and whispered to her, "No matter what happens, I want to thank you all for what you did for my father. I just called home and his fever has broken."

"That's wonderful, Pedro," Mindy said as she hugged him. "But I'm not surprised."

Pedro pushed her away. "We have to be careful," he said.

"Will we ever see you again?" she asked.

"I hope so. I'd like to hear more of what you've been saying."

"In case we don't see you again, I wish you'd promise me one thing. I wish you'd promise me that you'll continue to seek out God. If you seek Him, He will make Himself real to you," Mindy said with tears in her eyes.

"I think He already has."

Mr. Garcia stormed into the room. He looked angrily at Pedro. "You may leave now!"

The look on Mr. Garcia's face frightened Mindy.

"Pedro said we would get a fair trial," she said. "Let's get it over with."

"Don't worry. Your time will come."

"What have you done with Jeff?" Warren asked.

"He's on his way back to prison. He confessed to everything!"

# Chapter 18

# The Missing Video

That can't be!" Mindy snapped. "He's done nothing wrong!"

"Your brother said it was his decision alone to film Mr. Sanchez."

"That's not true! It was my idea," K.J. said.

"No, mine," Mindy said.

"Tell that to the judge," Mr. Garcia laughed. "And don't forget, you're not in America."

Warren walked over to Mr. Garcia. "I demand to see your superior immediately."

"Why?"

"I want to make a confession."

"You're all in a confessing mood now, aren't you?" Mr. Garcia said with a smile.

"I demand to see him now," Warren persisted.

Mr. Garcia picked up the phone and made a short call. Everyone waited in silence. K.J. stared at Mindy. Mindy stared at K.J. Then they both stared at Warren.

"What are you up to, Warren?" Mindy asked.

"Trust me," Warren whispered back.

Then the head of the secret police walked in.

"I understand someone wants to confess."

Warren took a piece of paper out of his pocket and handed it to him. "Sir, please phone this number. It's a news agency in Los Angeles."

"What does that have to do with your confession?" the official asked angrily.

"I confess that I'm aware of your trick. You knew all along that the tape got out of Cuba. You were just trying to bluff us with that phony tape."

The commander didn't confirm or deny it. "Get to the point."

"The point is that a news agency in the United States has the tape. They'll play it on stations across America if we are not released immediately."

"He's bluffing!" Mr. Garcia cried.

"Shut up and sit down," the commander said.

Mr. Garcia did as he was told.

K.J. and Mindy realized now why Warren had gone to the old hotel. He had made a phone call!

"If we release you all, will you give us the tape?"

"Sir, we didn't come here to cause trouble. We came to bring love, not embarrassment, to your nation. You have my word. Once we're back home, we will send you the tape."

There was silence while the commander considered his words.

"I have one more request," Warren said.

"What's that?"

"That you release Mr. Sanchez."

"We'll have to think about that one."

---

News spread rapidly that the team had been set free. In a few minutes, they would leave for the airport to fly home.

Pedro was with them as they rode the elevator down to the lobby. When the doors opened, they saw that the lobby was filled with cheering people.

As the Reel Kids made their way through the crowd, Jeff spotted Maria and Mr. Sanchez. He went over to hug them goodbye, and Mr. Sanchez told him that he had been released because of the evidence on the tape.

When they pulled away from the hotel entrance, Jeff turned around for one last look. Mindy waved farewell to Pedro, and K.J. filmed the crowd.

"So what did you think of your first trip, guys?" Jeff asked K.J. and Mindy.

"Awesome!" they said in unison.

"Amen!" Warren and Jeff agreed.

Other
# Reel Kids Adventures
by Dave Gustaveson

### The Missing Video
An exciting adventure into Communist Cuba. Will the dark-eyes stranger send the *Reel Kids* into an international nightmare?

### Mystery at Smokey Mountain
A spine-tingling mystery with the *Reel Kids* in the Philippines. Jeff and the "Reel Kids" become the target of wicked men as they attempt to help the poor at Smokey Mountain in Manila.

### The Stolen Necklace
A stolen necklace, wild animals and a life threatening African mystery will keep *Reel Kids* readers turning pages.

### The Mysterious Case
Jeff Caldwell couldn't imagine how one small mistake would cost them. A mysterious suitcase leads them on a collision course with the dangerous Colombian drug cartel. Would the drug lords allow them to continue their mission?

### The Amazon Stranger
The Reel Kids trip to South America had become far riskier than anyone could imagine. Would they escape the perils of the deadly river to reach the Amazon tribe?